A TOUCH OF CHRISTMAS MAGIC

A.D. ELLIS

CHAPTER 1
KAI DAVID JACKSON

"SHE'S PERFECT, KAI," HE WHISPERED GRUFFLY over the phone. At well past midnight, and even from over a thousand miles away, I could picture his light blue eyes sparkling with love for his new daughter.

Propping myself up against the headboard in my childhood home, I smiled and rubbed sleep from my eyes. I'd crashed after a long day at work, but Colby's calls were set to bypass any silent or mute feature on my phone.

My best friend since Kindergarten went on. "She's so pretty. The tiniest fingers and toes." He sniffed. "Like, how did I help make something so perfect and gorgeous?"

I kept myself from snorting, but all I could think was *Yeah, right. How did Colby Burke, the most gorgeous, amazing man I've ever known have anything to do with creating a perfect creature?* Instead, I rolled my eyes on my end of the phone in Peppermint Hollow, smack dab in the middle of Small Town, USA.

"And they're just going to let us walk out of here with her? Like what kind of system is this? I'm not trained to take a baby home." True worry laced Colby's words. I'd known the man since we were five and, twenty-five years later, I knew exactly the way the pale skin on his forehead crinkled when he was anxious about something. The way he'd be running his hand through his dishwater blond hair.

"You're going to be an amazing father," I said.

And I meant that with my entire being.

Colby had lived through and overcome a shitty childhood, and I knew he'd do everything in his power to make sure his baby never knew anything but love, support, and stability.

"I don't know," Colby hedged. "She's so amazing, and I know now what people mean about a baby being your heart on the outside of your body, but this wasn't part of the plan. Things with Mandy were such a shit show and," his words lowered, and I figured he wasn't alone, "Sasha and I aren't exactly talking forever." He sighed. "She's not doing well. At all."

My chest clenched.

My best friend had run from Peppermint Hollow years ago. Trying to escape his demons—even though he and his dad had a really good relationship *now*—and chasing happiness like a dog chomping at snowflakes. Just when he thought he'd found what he was looking for, it melted away.

After moving away from our hometown in the Midwest and settling in Florida, Colby had supposedly fallen for the love of his life. His first wife, Mandy, had ended up being an addict just like his mom. She cheated, nearly destroyed his business—CoJack Realty; *our* business—and trashed his heart.

I'd begged him to come home after he divorced Mandy, but Colby stubbornly stayed put, determined to earn love and happiness.

When he met Sasha and followed her to California while she looked for her next big break, my heart broke a tiny bit more.

I'd never *really* let myself believe Colby and I would become more than friends. Sure, we'd joked around the summer after our senior year that we'd give it a go if we were both still single when we were thirty. We'd been drinking and lounging together on the couch in my parents' basement, our limbs tangled together after we'd paused our wrestling match.

But the tipsy pact we'd made was nothing more than ramblings.

That was what my head kept telling me over the years.

My heart, however, had different hopes.

People always assumed we were a couple. We'd been joined at the hip since the first day of school. Colby spent more time at my house than he did his own—at least until his father, Thomas, pulled his shit together—and folks often joked that we were one person in two bodies.

They weren't wrong. Colby was my other half. A soul mate if ever there was one.

I had plenty of platonic friends of different genders. Being bisexual didn't mean I was destined to get all hot and bothered over my best friend.

But there I was.

I'd secretly longed for a chance to love Colby as more than a friend since we were about thirteen. But he'd never seen me that way—at least not for real. Sure, he joked that if he was ever going to go for a guy, it would be me, but Colby had always dated girls.

And he would have told me if he felt some sort of way for me.

Right?

I had to accept he wasn't looking to come home and fall for his best friend.

For the most part, I'd made peace with it.

Mostly.

But when he got with Sasha, it hurt. I guess a tiny part of me had hoped that the mess with Mandy would bring him home and we'd eventually joke about being thirty and single. We'd give the old high school pact a go.

Instead, he'd moved farther away and started playing house with another addict. Colby made jokes about always going for the only thing he knew, which meant unstable, unreliable addicts—something he had *a lot* of experience with thanks to his mother—but I knew it broke him a bit each time he ended up drawn to someone just like his mom.

And Sasha was definitely just like Colby's mom.

An addict.

Unreliable.

Unstable.

I think they did love each other in their own way for a short time, but I truly believe they would have broken up long ago if Sasha hadn't ended up pregnant.

Surprisingly, she'd committed to cleaning up her act for nine months. Colby had high hopes she'd stick with the new sobriety, but the fact Sasha had demanded a c-section to be scheduled as soon as possible had me thinking she was going right back to using as soon as the baby was born.

Imagining Colby and his baby leaving the hospital with a coked-out Sasha chilled my blood. *I should be with him. I should be helping. I should get to share this with my best friend.*

"What's her name?" I asked, steering Colby away from talk of Sasha. I wasn't sure my heart could handle hearing about how she was jonesing for a fix while my best friend cradled his new baby.

Colby took the distraction. "Elsie." I heard his smile across the miles. "Elsie Mae Burke."

"I want to see pictures," I said, emotions clogging my throat. "And don't even think about doing any work for at least a week. You know I've got it all covered."

CoJack Realty had been our brainchild during college. Colby and I were one and the same when it came to being able to turn on the charm and talk to pretty much anyone.

For me, that was my natural personality.

Friendly, outgoing, life of the party.

For Colby, it was more something he could flip on when needed.

He tended to be more broody, stand-off-ish, and quiet if given the chance.

Except around me.

We were the perfect mixture. We matched each other's energies, lifted and grounded when needed, and, as cliché as it sounds, truly completed each other.

Realty was something we were both interested in and good at.

We'd been CoJack since sixth grade when the teacher let us name our groups for a project, and the name had stuck. When it came to our business all those years later, there really wasn't any question about what we'd call ourselves.

CoJack Realty was successful beyond our wildest dreams. The business allowed us to set our hours, pad our savings accounts, work from wherever we wanted, and spend both at-home and at-work hours with our best friend.

"I'll send some as soon as I'm off the phone," Colby promised. The catch in his voice went straight to my heart. "Thanks for answering."

"Always. I'm here. You know that."

I'm here. For you, for Elsie, for us.

Always.

"Maybe you can come visit? See your new niece?" The unspoken *I don't want to be alone with a new baby and her addict mother* had me wondering how quickly I could book a flight to California.

"Of course. Say the word and I'm there."

Never mind Sasha hated me.

Or the fact seeing them together, bonding over their baby, building a life together—a life *I* wanted to share with Colby—would shred me.

If Colby needed me, I was there.

Always.

"Let me get everyone home and settled, then we'll make plans." Colby paused. "Listen, I think they're going to teach me how to give her a bottle here soon. Sasha refused to breastfeed her—" Bitterness crept into his words. "Won't even hold her or look at her really. So, the nurses said they had donated breastmilk, and they'd show me how to feed her."

I swallowed down the anger and disappointment

bubbling through me. "Fill her belly and let her know Uncle Kai loves her."

"Kai…" Colby's words cracked with emotion.

I waited.

"Fuck, Kai, I'm so scared. I don't know how to do this."

"You've got this, Cole. She's lucky to have you. Call me every hour of the day if you need to. Call your dad and Allison. Or my mom and dad." Thomas Burke and his longtime girlfriend, Allison, lived in Peppermint Hollow. My parents, Eric and Lacy Jackson, had recently moved to the retirement village. All four were friends, and I knew they'd jump in to help as needed. "We're all here for you. Always."

Colby sniffed and mumbled something along the lines of a goodbye.

The line went dead.

And my heart ached.

Ached for so many things.

Things I wished I could fix. Things I couldn't have. Things I wished were different.

But mostly, my heart ached because my other half was scared and hurting across the continent.

"She left," Colby said, his words flat.

We'd talked every day of our lives, and the last few months had been no different. As much as I'd wanted to go to him—offer my help, ease him into fatherhood…as if I knew anything about being a parent—I'd held off.

In the first week after Elsie Mae was born, Colby held

out hope Sasha was turning over a new leaf. She wanted nothing to do with the baby, and she was never seen without a drink in hand, but she hadn't shown any signs of drug use.

By week two, everything had changed.

"She's gone all day," Colby had said, his words ragged with exhaustion. "When she comes home in the evening, she doesn't even look at Elsie. Just crashes. She leaves again in the early morning hours."

"Where does she go?"

He'd sighed. "No idea. I really don't even care. Mostly, I just want her away from Elsie; I know she's volatile when she's using." Desperation laced his words, and I imagined him paralyzed by indecision. Leave his baby's mother? Stick around and face the inevitable harm Sasha would bring to Elsie—whether physically or emotionally?

"So, the drugs are back?" I hadn't been surprised, but my heart hurt for Colby.

"New track marks. She doesn't even try to hide them." The tiny baby noises on the other end of the phone brought a smile to my face. "I know I need to get Elsie away from her—and I would in a heartbeat if she was around more than she is," he'd said when we'd spoken earlier in the week.

Elsie Mae was four months old and thriving. As much as things with Colby and Sasha sucked, Colby as a father was rockin' it as I'd predicted. He'd yet to feel out the idea of putting her in daycare or getting a nanny, working his hours around her naps and bottles.

Now, his words registered. "Left? Like moved out?" I asked.

"Yeah. One day last week, she was showered, dressed

up, and headed out the door at a regular time." His chuckle held only bitterness. "My stupid ass thought for one split second she'd gotten a job or something." Sasha had dreams of being an actress, but nothing had ever panned out.

"Then today," Colby went on, "she comes in while I'm feeding Elsie. Two suitcases and a big handbag. Hands me a brown envelope as she cries. 'I'm sorry,' she says. 'I'm not a mother. I won't do to her what my mother did to me. I'm sorry for what we ended up, but there's no one I'd trust more to be her daddy.' Then she walked out." Colby sniffled. "The envelope had a short note saying she was leaving the country. She'd met someone who could offer her a chance at more." He scoffed. "More coke most likely. Anyway, there was a thick sheaf of papers. She'd signed them."

"Like divorce? But you weren't married."

"Termination of parental rights. She signed papers saying she was no longer the parent of our baby." Colby's words caught. "I don't know if I'm more pissed or relieved."

"And they're legit?" My heart played tug-of-war with my emotions. Anguish and hope.

"Yeah, I sent them to our attorney. He said they looked legit but shared them with a friend in family law. They're legally sound."

"So, what does this mean?"

Colby laughed bitterly. "I'm a single dad without an addict living in my apartment. Pretty much nothing changed other than now I don't have to worry about her being around Elsie."

"Come home," I blurted out.

"What?"

I imagined Colby with Elsie propped on his shoulder as he burped her—I'd seen him do it during our daily video chats—his blue eyes squinting.

"Come home," I repeated.

"I don't have a place there. I can't just show up in town with a baby. Dad and Allison are in an apartment. Not enough room for me and Elsie."

"Don't be a dumbass. Move in with me. I've got plenty of room."

Never mind that the only room with a bed right now was the master bedroom. When Mom and Dad moved to the Peppermint Hollow Retirement Village, I'd jumped at the chance to make my childhood home my own.

They'd agreed to sell to me, and I'd helped them move the furniture they wanted to keep to their new place.

As much as I loved the old house, I got rid of most of the furniture and décor they didn't want and planned to slowly furnish and decorate it as I desired.

Some of the more sentimental pieces were moved to the basement, but many of the rooms were empty or close to it—I hadn't brought a lot with me from my tiny apartment on the outskirts of town.

My new bed in the master bedroom was king-size. Colby and I were both about six-foot-two, fairly average height and build, and could easily share until he got his own room set up.

Or he could just share with me indefinitely. Not like we hadn't slept together a million times growing up.

But that was all something we could discuss once I got him back home.

"I don't know. I don't want to risk Elsie getting any

kind of crud on an airplane. Plus, I'd have stuff I'd want to bring, so a road trip would be better than a flight. But driving cross-country with an infant?" He sighed. "I don't know that I have it in me. Would that even be good for her?"

"She'd be with her daddy. Safe, fed, warm, and loved. Nowhere else better." I meant the words. Elsie struck gold with Colby as her father, and I'd spend the rest of our lives making sure he believed just how amazing he was.

"It sounds like hell," Colby hedged.

"But?" I knew when my best friend was wavering.

He huffed out an exasperated breath. "There's nothing here for me. Never really has been. I can't say I miss small-town living, but damn, I miss everyone."

"Then it's settled."

"Wait, I didn't say that. There's a lot of logistics to figure out." The sound of his words changed, and I imagined him walking from one room to another. Water running told me he was likely rinsing a bottle in the sink.

"I'll come out and help pack. We'll make the trip back together." I already had visions of hooking a U-Haul to Colby's big black truck and making a week of traveling back home. Me, my best friend, his baby girl. My heart squeezed in my chest.

Colby was quiet for a long time. "I'll think about it."

A terrible gurgling noise filled the line.

"Um, what was that?"

He groaned. "Oh my god, I've got to go. She just exploded. It's running down my arm."

The line went dead.

Exploded?

Puke? Poop?

Images of an exploded baby filled my head. What was running down his arm?

Was that something I wanted to get involved in? Could I even handle a baby, let alone the near disasters that came with one?

My heart thumped double-time.

If it meant getting Colby back by my side and helping him raise his baby, I'd deal with whatever bodily fluids and explosions Elsie wanted to bring my way.

I just needed my best friend back home.

CHAPTER 2

COLBY GARRISON BURKE

A DAY AFTER KAI PUT THAT STUPID IDEA IN MY head about going home, I'd nearly gone insane thinking about it.

We'd need to drive. I wasn't putting a baby on an airplane. Sure, millions of infants had traveled by plane and been fine, but I wasn't taking a chance of Elsie getting some type of creepin' crud being blown through the ventilation system.

I maybe didn't know everything there was to know about parenting, but I knew enough to avoid things that just didn't feel good for my baby and me. I'd only been a father for four months, but gut instinct had served me well so far and I was proud as hell that Elsie was healthy and meeting every milestone all the books said she should be meeting.

I knew *I* didn't have much to do with that, but I still breathed a sigh of relief when checkups went well, and she did something a checklist said she was supposed to.

Shit.

Speaking of checkups, I'd need to find a new pediatrician if we moved.

I thought of the sterile, professional-if-not-welcoming doctor's office I took Elsie to now.

Yeah, I definitely wasn't going to miss that place.

Peppermint Hollow had a small family practice, and the larger town up the road was home to the county hospital and other doctors. I had no doubt I could find good care for my baby back home.

Getting there was the biggest negative if I was being honest.

Driving from California back to Peppermint Hollow? It would be a thirty-hour drive, which we obviously wouldn't be doing all in one go. If it was just me, I could probably do eight to ten hours a day and make the drive in about three days. But I wasn't going to push it that hard with Elsie in tow. We could drive six or so hours a day and make it a comfortable week-long trip.

Not a trip I'd want to do by myself with Elsie, but if Kai wanted to come help, it wouldn't be so bad.

My heart had always tugged me back toward my hometown, but I'd spent years and years ignoring that pull. Now though? I wasn't sure my reasons for leaving were as structurally sound as the reason for going back.

I'd left Peppermint Hollow for a million reasons.

The biggest one being my mom. Trying to outrun the demons she'd left me with. Trying to find the sense of family and happiness I never had as a kid.

Actually, that's not true. I had family and happiness with the Jacksons. I spent as much time as possible at Kai's house, soaking up all the goodness. As if it would protect me from the disappointment of my addict mother and my detached father.

My dad and I had something good *now*, and I'd been strangely relieved when my mom passed away in my early twenties, but my home life as a child had left *a lot* to be desired.

I hadn't found what I was looking for in those other places I'd run to. Only the same heartache and unworthiness I'd been trying to escape.

I'd grown a lot in the years since I'd been away from Peppermint Hollow. I knew myself better and I'd worked through some of the demons Mom left me with.

Some of them, not all. I was definitely a work in progress.

The other reason I'd left home was my best friend.

Kai David Jackson.

The most amazing soul I'd ever had the pleasure of knowing.

So, why would I leave him and go chasing after impossible dreams?

Why, indeed?

We made this pact way back at the end of high school. We'd been drinking and wrestling as per our norm that summer—and pretty much every day since we'd met and become fast friends. Tangled up with him on the couch, pausing to catch our breaths, every single impossible hope I'd ever given space to in my brain regarding Kai and me being more than best friends glommed together into a half-baked idea.

The words had spilled out of me before I had time to think them through.

"If we're still single by the time we're thirty, let's get together and give it a shot."

With his pale skin flushing pink, Kai's big hazel eyes stared up at me, searching my face, trying to see if I was serious.

Forget the fact I'd secretly wondered about my sexuality—at least where Kai was concerned—for most of our senior year, and maybe even before that. I wasn't exactly sure when my thoughts had switched from loving Kai as my best bro to still loving him as my best bro but wanting to touch him and be with him in very non-best-bro ways.

I liked girls. I did. But I loved Kai; I was drawn to him in a way that made absolutely no sense. But at the same time, the feelings I had for my best friend were the only things that made sense in my heart.

Instead of high school me letting Kai know right then and there that I maybe kinda wanted to see what things would be like between us, I'd shrugged. "I mean, by the time we're thirty, we'll have lived enough life. If we're single, maybe we just give in to what everyone thinks anyway."

Lame.

So lame.

Looking back, I wanted to kick my own ass. I should have just told him. We could have given it a shot and become something great.

Or we could have crashed and burned and lost our friendship.

Plus, if I'd told him, I likely wouldn't have Elsie.

But memories of that day on the couch still haunted me.

Kai swallowed and nodded, shoving his light brown hair from his eyes. "Yeah, sure. Thirty." Then he'd punched me in the gut. "Not like either of us will be single by then anyway."

The wrestling had picked back up and life had marched on through the hot, muggy Midwestern summer.

College, setting up CoJack Realty, daily chats, everything was completely normal, just as best friends should be.

We'd only mentioned the pact from time to time over the years. Always as a joke, always as if there was no way we'd ever get to that point.

Always as if neither of us *wanted* to get to that point.

But I was thirty and single.

A single *father*. Was there a clause in the pact for that?

Was it fair of me to bring my latent bisexual feelings into the picture? And maybe I was more *Kai*-sexual than anything. Truly, I could appreciate *any* hot guy, but the actual attraction to and deep-down feelings for a man only rang true for me with Kai if I was being honest.

So, yeah, it wasn't fair of me to bring these feelings I'd had for so many years, along with a *baby*, to Kai's doorstep.

I'd left Peppermint Hollow to escape my mom and to keep my feelings out of my friendship. If Kai had felt anything for me all these years, he would have brought it up, right? I mean, he talked plenty about guys and girls he found attractive. Told me about dates, bits and pieces about sex—just kill me now—and the eventual breakups.

Did it make me an asshole that I always felt relief when Kai and whatever guy or girl he was dating parted ways? Yeah, probably. I'd moved across the country to follow women I had absolutely no business being with, swearing to my best friend that I loved them, but my heart thrilled each and every time I knew Kai was single again.

Ass.

Hole.

Kai was bisexual. If he'd had even a fraction of the feelings for me that I had for him, he would have told me.

Like you told him?

I shook off the thought.

We'd talked every damn day of our lives since Kindergarten. We'd spent whole days, weeks, months together during the quarter-century-plus we'd known each other. We worked side-by-side day in and day out—whether we were together physically or thousands of miles apart—at CoJack Realty.

I would have known.

Or he would have said something.

And I wasn't going to fuck up our friendship by admitting my feelings. It was better to pine silently and keep Kai as my best friend than to risk losing him.

I glanced around the apartment I'd called home since moving to California with Sasha. There was absolutely no attachment to the place. Moving home had been the last thing I ever thought I'd do, but the thought of Peppermint Hollow, being close to family and friends, raising Elsie in my hometown, it was *all* I could think about now.

Elsie finished her bottle, and I moved her to my shoulder to burp her. With any luck, I wouldn't end up wearing formula or baby poop today. "What do you say, Else? Wanna go meet your grandparents and Uncle Kai?"

A sharp pang gripped my heart. Kai was so much more

than *Uncle*. Sure, we were closer than some brothers, but I wanted him to be more to my baby.

More to *me*.

Maybe it was crazy, but it was what my soul craved.

I'd need to keep a tight lid on that shit; I wasn't headed home to fuck things up with my best friend.

Kai's early-morning call brought a smile to my face. He was as excited about me coming home as I was. "Well? Can I buy my ticket? Are we making a road trip home?"

I glanced to where Elsie slept after a butt-crack-of-dawn bottle. Was there anything for my daughter and me here? Any reason to stay a thousand miles away from my best friend and family? Let my daughter grow up only knowing her family from pictures and video calls and once-a-year trips to visit?

Aside from the conviction of *knowing* I needed to keep my feelings for Kai secret, there was no *real* reason for me to stay away from Peppermint Hollow anymore. Several of the demons of my past were still with me, despite running across the country. Working through what my mom left me with could be done just as well—maybe even easier—back home. Allowing my dad and I to continue building the relationship we'd missed out on when I was a kid—and letting him have a second chance to get it right as a grandfather—appealed to the child in my soul who longed for a functional family.

Elsie squirmed, her cute little nose scrunching and a tiny fist flailing. She'd wake soon and I'd be inundated with diapers, bottles, tummy time, and a million work-related things when I got her to nap.

Suddenly, I felt very tired and very alone.

I wanted my best friend.

"Yeah." My words hitched. "Yeah. Get your ticket."

"Yes!"

"Kai?"

"Yeah?"

"Hurry."

Kai hesitated. "You okay, man?"

"Yeah. I just miss you. Want you to meet Elsie. And, now that I've decided to do it, I just want to get home."

"I'm buying my ticket as we speak."

Three days later, the apartment was empty except for a suitcase, the diaper bag, Elsie's pack-n-play, boxes of clothing for both of us, the solid oak, handmade kitchen table and chairs I couldn't stand to part with—I'd bought it when I moved to California because I couldn't help but think about how much Kai would love it—and my recliner.

I smiled when I looked at the old chair.

Kai and I bought matching recliners in college. Those crap chairs had gotten us through four years, but they'd fallen apart not long after graduation. With our first big paycheck at CoJack Realty, we'd splurged and bought top-of-the-line matching recliners.

The chair had gone with me from Peppermint Hollow to Florida to California. It had become Elsie's favorite place to rock as I prayed for her to fall asleep. And it was where I felt closest to Kai. Sure, we talked every day. I saw his pretty hazel eyes and killer smile on video calls multiple times a day.

But at the end of a long day, especially when Elsie was super fussy—what was it with babies and that certain chunk of time I'd come to think of as *the witching hour*? Or was that just my baby? —I'd sink into that chair with Elsie snuggled against my chest and imagine the soft upholstery was Kai's arms holding me close.

I was so fucking screwed.

Kai's flight was on time, and he was in an Uber heading toward me from the airport. I'd told the twin brothers who lived down the hall I'd give them a hundred bucks each if they'd help with loading the U-Haul. Their mom had offered to watch Elsie, but I hadn't been able to bring myself to let her out of my sight.

So, I kept my daughter cuddled to my chest as I watched out the window. Kai and I had been sharing locations on our phones ever since the feature became a thing. He was supposedly only minutes away.

"Mr. Burke," Desmond called from down the hall. "We're here to help." His brother, Dwayne followed him.

"And I'll hold that precious baby while you all load the trailer," their mother, Alicia said with a knowing smile. "I won't move away from where you can see me, but I think that table will take all four of you to get it out the door."

Blushing, I gave a nod. "Thanks, appreciate it."

Alicia smiled. "I remember what it's like to have a brand-new baby."

I glanced at the two gangly teen boys and cocked a brow. "Can't imagine having two; and the teen years?" I pretended to shiver. Elsie was a tiny bundle in my arms. She was barely four months old, had already outgrown her newborn clothes, was over the fiftieth percentile in weight —only the twenty-fifth percentile in height, which made sense because Sasha was very short as was my own mother. No way my little baby would ever be a teen. Or dating. Or driving. Or going off to college.

Oh god.

My heart clenched.

"It goes by in the blink of an eye," Alicia said with a sympathetic smile. "The good thing is that it also somehow has a way of going at just the right speed. Each new phase is exciting and exhausting and has you so tangled up that you barely have time to think about the phases they've outgrown."

I wanted to build a blanket fort and hide away with Elsie, protecting her and my heart forever.

A sleek black sports car rolled up to the curb out front.

I knew without a doubt that it was Kai because, of course, he'd get an Uber in some fancy-ass car just because he could.

Alicia and her boys became background noise as I beelined it out the door.

Kai was out of the car, a suitcase and duffle on the ground beside him, and a gleam in his eyes that matched the pure gold in his smile.

Oh my god, I loved this man so damn much.

I didn't know how I was going to live with him and not fall at his feet begging him to touch me, love me. But how I'd survived without him within arm's reach for all these years was beyond me.

Tears stung my eyes as Kai walked straight into my arms. We'd shared a million hugs in our lifetime, but this one had been too long coming and held a shit-ton of emotion. We laughed into each other's shoulders, slapping each other's backs, until we finally just gripped fistfuls of shirt and held on as if the world was ending.

He'd come.

Kai had dropped everything and come here to rescue me.

And that was only one of the million things that made him amazing.

Elsie squirmed and made a snuffling noise against my chest.

"Oh my god, did I hurt her?" Kai's stricken face was hilarious.

"No, she's fine. Just grunty when she gets disturbed."

Kai leaned in and pressed a kiss to the downy-soft hair on Elsie's head. "Hello, Elsie Mae. Uncle Kai is here and we're going to be the best of friends."

My heart nearly clawed its way from my chest right there on the sidewalk.

"I want to hold her so badly," Kai said, rubbing his hand over her back, "but let's get everything loaded first. Then I can wash up. I feel gross from the plane."

I introduced Kai to Alicia, Desmond, and Dwayne before handing a still-sleeping Elsie over to Alicia. She nodded and winked as she tucked the baby close. "I'll be right here."

The twins, Kai, and I had the U-Haul loaded in under an hour. Once Kai and I had the U-Haul hooked to my big black Ram 1500 truck, I paid the boys, took Elsie back from Alicia, and thanked them.

"You have my number if you're ever in the Midwest. Peppermint Hollow isn't exactly a touristy spot, but you're always welcome to come visit." I shook hands with the boys and let Alicia give me a hug.

"Looks like you've got yourself a good one there," she whispered.

I started to pretend like I had no clue what she was talking about. Instead, I glanced at Kai as he hefted his luggage into the truck. "Yeah," I said. "He's the best." For the first time in my life, I was admitting—ever so slightly —to someone other than myself that I had more than friendship feelings for my best friend.

"Don't let him get away. I lost a true love because I was too stubborn and full of pride to admit my love." She watched her boys as they headed back inside. "I don't regret what I had with their father, but Leanna was something special and my heart hurts every day that I lost her because I couldn't see what was right in front of me."

I nodded; my throat too choked with emotion to speak. And then she turned and followed her boys. I had a feeling Alicia was one of those people who come into your life right when you most need them; her words hit me deep.

"Show me the soap," Kai crowed. "I've got a baby to hold."

I'd left one towel, soap, shampoo, and clothes out of my packing for Kai—knowing the man for as many years as I had, I knew he wouldn't have thought to bring clothes to change into after a shower. "There's underwear, sweats, and a t-shirt on the sink." We'd shared clothes so much through the years, I sometimes wondered if we ever actually knew who owned what. Luckily, we wore the same sizes and liked the same casual look. Jeans, t-shirts, joggers, fashion sneakers, or work boots. Throw in a flannel or hoodie if it was cold; a button-up or light sweater if we needed to dress things up a bit.

I smiled as I thought of the time we had to do shirts

and ties for headshots for CoJack Realty. I didn't think either of us had worn that shit since the photo shoot, but we'd looked pretty damn good at the time.

While Kai showered, I fixed Elsie the last bottle she'd ever drink in the apartment and made sure her car seat was ready. We'd do a diaper change after a good burp and be good to go for a fairly long stretch. That was the good thing about tiny babies—they didn't do a whole lot other than eat, poop, and sleep. I hadn't *known* this going into fatherhood, but I'd learned it quickly. Traveling with a small infant would actually be a lot easier than traveling with a toddler.

Kai emerged from the bathroom in a cloud of steam, smelling like my soap, and my gut clenched. After running the towel through his damp hair, he tossed it back toward the bathroom, not paying attention to it landing in a heap —some things hadn't changed at all—and rubbed his hands together. "Gimme the baby," he said in a silly voice that warmed my heart.

"Have you ever held a baby?" I asked.

"Shut up, don't act like you were a top-notch baby-holder before this beauty was born. My mom assures me I won't break her unless I really try." My eyes widened in horror and Kai laughed. "Not that I'd *try*. God man, your face." He sat on the floor and made grabby hands.

I retrieved the bottle and joined him, both of us leaning against the wall. "Main thing—and it's easier to do with a pillow, but you can use my knee—is to support her head. She's wobbly." I handed my heart over to the man I'd loved in one way or another for twenty-five years. Elsie stretched and fussed.

"Oh shit, she doesn't like me."

I laughed. "She's hungry and she doesn't like to be woken up." Pausing, I stared at my daughter in Kai's arms and tried to sort through the emotions. Awe, slight jealousy, extreme love that couldn't be explained, and the most heart-wrenching feeling of *rightness* I'd ever experienced.

Clearing my throat as Elsie's fusses got a bit louder, I held the bottle out to him. "Girl knows how to chug a bottle, so this part should be easy. We'll get to diaper changes next."

Kai took the bottle and held it to Elsie's mouth, smiling up at me proudly when she latched on and went to town. "I've been practicing diapers."

My jaw dropped. "What? How?"

"Got a doll and been watching videos. Mom helped too." He spoke to me, but his eyes never left Elsie as she sucked down her lunch. "I got this cool baby wrap thing too. I met this lady at the class she taught at the hospital, and she fitted me with the right one. I've only tried it with the doll, but it lets you hold her close and have both hands free—we can both use it since we're the same height and all. Oh, I've got a person coming to show us all we need to do to baby-proof the house—since it's old, I figured we'd need assistance. Do you have one of those baby monitors with the video? I figure she won't need her own room right away, but I got the monitor because it was the highest rated in the safety category. I like that we can hear her and see her from anywhere in the house." Kai glanced up and continued. "Had the pipes tested for lead. Put a water filtration system in. Got a humidifier since old houses have dry air. And when it gets closer, we'll make sure to have the best Baby's First Christmas *ever*."

I couldn't speak.

"What?" Kai asked as tears stung my eyes.

I sniffed. Having a damn baby had made me more emotional than I'd ever been.

Having a best friend you're in love with step in and act as if co-parenting with you is the most natural thing in the world also has you wrecked.

No lies detected.

"Just impressed," I said. "That's a lot of extra you didn't have to do. I appreciate it."

He took the bottle from Elsie and set it aside. "Anything for this girl." He bumped his shoulder into mine. "And her daddy. Now, show me how to burp her. But I don't want her to, like, puke on me or anything."

I laughed. "Attempt at your own risk."

"Seriously?" Kai asked, his nose wrinkled in distaste.

"I can burp her. It's usually a forty-sixty chance you'll get more than a burp."

"No." Kai took a deep breath. "I've got this."

I'd known the man since we were five. I knew enough to know when he was determined to do something. So, I showed him how to get her up on his shoulder and how to pat the burp out of her. The way he froze in fear when the tiny bundle burped as loud as a frat brother, waiting for the explosion of puke, made me chuckle.

"Looks like you dodged the mess this time."

"Dude, she burped like she'd just done a keg-stand," Kai exclaimed, his eyes wide before he busted out laughing.

"Just wait until she farts."

We fell against each other, laughing until we could barely breathe.

"Thank you," I whispered. "For coming. For bringing me home. Bringing both of us home."

"Always."

CHAPTER 3

KAI

I COULD BARELY BREATHE, AND MY HEART wanted to explode out of my chest.

Everything I'd felt for Colby had intensified ten-fold and I wasn't sure I'd survive.

From age five to thirteen, he was my everything. My ride or die. The person I wanted to spend every waking moment with. He made me laugh, made me feel loved, and made me a better person.

The other half of my soul.

From thirteen on, all of that remained the same, but I added in romantic feelings. And then, when hormones hit hard around sixteen, sexual feelings sprouted and multiplied.

But nothing in this world could have prepared me for seeing Colby with a baby.

My baby.

I knew it sounded demented, but Elsie owned as much of my heart as her father did, and I'd thought of her as *mine* from the moment he told me Sasha was pregnant.

I hadn't let myself *admit* it until Colby said Sasha signed away her parental rights.

I was setting myself up for soul-crushing heartache when Colby eventually found someone he wanted to settle down with. Someone he wanted to build his little family with. Someone who definitely wouldn't be me.

Oh god, I couldn't breathe.

But for the time being, I let myself soak up how amazing and *right* it felt to be next to Colby and holding Elsie.

"Okay, Elsie Mae, you ready to be my first ever real-life diaper change?" I asked the baby, her eyes bright as they watched me. Glancing at Colby, I frowned. "I'm not sure she's okay with me. She's just staring."

He smiled. "You're a new face. New hair color, new eyes. Even your scruff is a different shade. She's learning you." He brushed a finger down his daughter's chunky little cheek. "Pretty sure she's fascinated with you. She probably recognizes your voice from the video calls and now she's got you right here in front of her."

I pouted. "I wanted to make her smile."

Colby leaned into me, pressing his head aside mine as he looked at the baby, then he stood up and took her from me. "She only started smiling at me like a week or so ago. Give her a bit to warm up."

I let him pull me up to stand. "Can I opt out of the diaper if it's poop? I've been practicing, but I'm not ready for that."

"Nope," Colby said, popping the p. "Think I got to wait until it wasn't poop? This is baptism by fire. Throwing you into the deep end and see if you can swim."

The look on my face must have shown the pure terror in my soul because the asshole laughed.

"I'll be right there to help, promise." He nestled Elsie in her car seat. We let her babble and coo as she batted at the black and white toys hanging from the car seat handle. Colby got a few tiny smiles. I still got nothing, but she watched me like she was interested.

Colby played with her tiny toes. "It's best to keep her upright like this for a while after she eats. If she lays flat, she'll spit up. She'll probably fill her diaper in a few minutes. Then we can change her and hit the road."

Sure enough, Elsie's precious little face turned beet red about ten minutes later and the worst gurgling sound filled the air.

"Uh-oh, that one sounded like it may have been a blow-out." His words sounded slightly stressed.

"What's a blow-out?"

"Like it somehow barely even touches the diaper and ends up all up her back and leaking from around her legs." He grimaced and moved to his knees. "I didn't keep any other clothes out for her. May have to go dig for another onesie." Moving the car seat handle out of the way, he lifted her up and showed me the baby's back. "You see any poop?"

"Oh god," I whispered as I inspected her. "No? I don't think so."

"Okay, we may have lucked out. Let's get her changed."

I watched in awe as Colby spread the towel I'd used out on the floor. "We're not taking this with us. Might as well risk it rather than her blanket. Okay, here we go." He grabbed the diaper, wipes, and diaper cream and gestured for me to get started.

"Oh god," I whispered.

We both knelt in front of the squirmy infant, who was now cooing and smiling up a storm as she kicked her little legs.

"How is she so happy sitting in shit?" I asked.

Colby threw his head back and laughed. "This will only last for a moment. She'll get super crabby if we don't change her."

I took a deep breath.

And almost gagged.

"Oh god, that's bad." I pulled my shirt up over my nose. "I'm gonna puke."

"Pull it together, man. Don't forget, we lived together long enough, I know how badly you can blow up a bathroom."

I unsnapped the little onesie Elsie wore and let Colby help move it up and out of the way.

"Here, get the other diaper ready," he said as he spread out the clean diaper. "And have some wipes pulled out."

I undid the diaper and moved it slightly to check on the damage. "Oh god," I whisper-moaned. "Why can't I start with just pee?"

Colby chuckled. "Come on, the longer she sits in it, the more likely she could get a rash."

"Oh shit." I snorted. "Literally." Grabbing a chunk of wipes, I grabbed her feet like I'd practiced and lifted up her little butt. Wiping away the mess the best I could, I tossed the disgusting mass into the old diaper like Mom had suggested.

"Dude, I'm not strapped for cash, but wipes aren't cheap. You can use one at a time."

I glanced at Colby to see if he was joking.

He wasn't.

Finishing the job without a fistful of wipes, I let go of Elsie's feet and went to work wrapping up the whole mess in the dirty diaper. The baby kicked and cooed. Colby inspected my work.

"What? Didn't think I could do it?"

He shrugged. "Considering you almost gagged and that wasn't even a bad one, I had my doubts." Laughing at my irritation, he lifted her legs and pointed at the top of the tiniest butt crack I'd ever seen. "When I first started changing her, I'd miss way up here. You got it all though. Good job."

Elsie continued to churn her little legs and make happy noises.

"She likes being naked, huh?"

Colby grinned. "Loves bath time and having her diaper off. I'd guess it feels good to get cool air on her skin."

"She get rashes a lot?" I picked up the tube of diaper rash stuff. "Butt Paste? Couldn't have gone with a nicer name?"

"Nurses at the hospital suggested it. It's good stuff. Keeps her skin from getting raw when she's wet or dirty." He checked his watch. "Let's go ahead and get her ready so we can hit the road. Hold out a finger; gonna give you more than I'd usually use, but only because she'll be in the car seat longer than usual."

I grimaced as I smeared on the paste, grunting when one of Elsie's little feet plopped right into the glob of diaper rash cream. "Oh god, she's getting it everywhere."

Colby laughed. "It's okay, it won't hurt her. And it doesn't stain or anything." He wiped her heel and a smear of cream on her thigh. "Finish up."

Cleaning my finger with a wipe first, I grabbed Elsie's feet again and lifted her to slide the diaper underneath. Colby helped get the position right and I pulled up the front before securing the tabs.

Colby inspected my work again—I felt like a kid trying to pass my driving exam or something. "Looks good. You'll be a pro in no time."

As stupid as it sounds, I couldn't help the proud thrill coursing through me at his words.

He snapped her onesie into place and held her against his chest, kissing her head and cuddling her while whispering nonsense. Then he put her into her car seat and got her snuggled in. After clipping a pacifier to her shirt and tucking a blanket around her legs, he hefted the carrier into the crook of his elbow.

As we stood in the middle of his apartment, I wondered if he had special memories he'd struggle to leave behind.

Almost like he read my mind, Colby took a deep breath. "Not gonna miss this place at all. I brought her home here, but it's never meant anything for real." Glancing down at his baby, he smiled. "Ready to get home and make some real memories, Else?"

She cooed and tried to kick off the blanket.

With the baby carrier on one arm and his other arm thrown around my shoulder, Colby ushered me toward the door. "Time to hit the road."

He showed me how to snap her car seat into the base —four doors on the truck made it a lot easier than I'd imagined—and how the mirror worked so he could see her face while he drove. "She'll sleep for a long stretch now that she's eaten and has a clean diaper. Figure we'll drive until she wakes up. Play it by ear whether we stop for the night or feed her and try to move on."

Climbing into Colby's sleek, black truck, I nodded. "I'm yours for the whole week. We can do our work from anywhere. No need to push her; if we need to stop, we stop." Glancing back at Elsie, I frowned. "Should I sit back there with her?"

"Nah, she's seriously just gonna sleep. Look at those sleepy eyes already." He adjusted his mirror and smiled at his baby. "She'll be out before we're on the freeway."

Elsie was a master napper and slept for an entire four hours before making a fuss. Colby and I chatted the whole way—about work, our families, home, Elsie, and random shit that only two best friends could turn into conversation.

We opted to feed her, change her, let her stretch, and play a bit, and then made another two hours before pulling into a hotel.

"It's not a five-star, but it should be clean. There's food next door." He pointed to a restaurant and a couple fast-food places. "This work for you?"

"I'm good with wherever as long as we can eat, shower, and sleep."

Once Elsie was stretched out in her pack-n-play next to the bed—Colby hadn't even batted an eyelash when the clerk said they had a king-size bed available, so I just went with it—I flopped down with a groan.

"I saw a gym area when we came in," Colby said. "You

care if I go run a mile and then I'll shower and get us food?"

I'd always loved when we ran together, and part of me wanted to follow him down and take the second treadmill.

Duh.

I couldn't leave the baby.

Damn, this parenting thing took some getting used to.

"No problem," I said, sitting up and looking at Elsie. "What if she cries?"

"She shouldn't. She's happy for now."

I eyed him with doubt and Colby laughed. "*For now* is my concern."

"Pick her up, talk to her, distract her, try holding her close, try laying her on the bed, give her the pacifier." He leaned down into the pack-n-play and let Elsie squeeze his finger as she cooed. "It won't take me long to run a mile."

"Go for two if you need to. I'll run in the morning." I moved to stand next to him.

Colby stood up straight and took a step toward me. For one crazy second, I thought he was going to kiss me. Instead, he just pulled me into a hug. "Thank you. For giving me time to run, for being here, for loving her."

"Always," I said against his shoulder, worried the catch in my words would betray my emotions. *I will always be here. Loving you. Loving her like she's my own.*

When Colby was changed and out the door, I leaned over the edge of Elsie's little bed. "Hey there, pretty girl." What was it about babies that automatically had people talking like fools? But her eyes latched onto me, and she kicked and cooed, happy just to be out of her seat if I had to bet. "You good down there?" I eyed the bed. I could play with her more easily up at my level, but would that be asking for trouble? She seemed happy where she was.

I opted to take the chance. Bound and determined to get her to smile at me—or at least get her used to me enough that a smile *might* happen—I hoisted her up into my arms. Careful to support her head, I moved to lay her down, but Elsie snuggled into my shoulder, and I couldn't help the huge-ass grin I gave my reflection as I watched in the mirror.

Did I think she was purposely cuddling into me? No. But she didn't cry, and she looked damn perfect all snug against my chest. If I had the baby wrap unpacked, I would have tried it right then and there.

But it was playtime, so I placed her gently on the bed and sat cross-legged at her feet so I could see her. Colby assured me she wasn't rolling yet, so I didn't have to worry about her face-planting off the bed.

Elsie and I enjoyed our get-to-know-each-other time immensely. Well, I did, and I was pretty sure she did. Hints of smiles played at her little mouth, but nothing full-blown.

Not yet.

When Colby came through the door, I realized he'd been gone thirty minutes.

He eyed us on the bed. "Did she cry?"

"No, just thought it was easier to play with her if she was up here. I didn't leave her alone, even if she's not rolling."

Colby shook his head with a smile. "I trust you."

"But I've got to pee," I said, moving to stand from the bed. "She's yours for one minute." Leaving the bathroom door open as I peed, I called out. "I've been reading this book, *What to Expect the First Years*. I got it after *What to Expect When You're Expecting*—which was *a lot* of information I'm not sure I really wanted to know."

Walking back into the room, I found Colby sitting on the bed, the scent of hand sanitizer hanging in the air, and his big hand on Elsie's tiny belly. But his jaw hung open and his eyes locked on me.

"What?"

"You read *What to Expect When You're Expecting*?"

I shrugged. "Sure. My best friend was going through a surprise pregnancy with a woman he wasn't one hundred percent sold on. Figured I could take the journey with him, even if it was silently from afar."

Colby swallowed and shook his head. After a moment, he cleared his throat. "That book...yeah, it was a lot. Sasha didn't like it. She got pissed any time I referred to it."

"This one...the first years one...it's easier to read. Not as overwhelming. But it's got a lot of good information. Shit I never would have guessed in a million years."

"Agreed." He stared at me again before glancing away as if to clear his head. "If you'll call in an order while I shower, I'll go get the food."

"Sounds good."

"You can totally shower while she's in the pack-n-play."

I eyed him dubiously.

"For real. I usually stick her in her car seat on the floor of the bathroom while I shower. If not, I'd never get anything done."

Once the food was ordered and a freshly showered Colby headed out the door, I looked from the baby bed to the bathroom. With Elsie in one arm, I made use of the wheels on her little cage and moved it to the bathroom door. I'd be able to see her from the shower if she cried.

She didn't make a peep while I took the fastest shower ever.

As I was pulling on sweats, the door clicked, but caught on the baby bed.

"What the fuck?" Colby mumbled.

"Sorry, sorry." I rushed toward the door with a sheepish grin. "Sorry. I moved her over here so I could see her if she cried while I was taking a shower."

Colby just smirked and shook his head. "Glad to see you're as gone over the tiny human as I am."

"Right? How does one little person capture a heart so fast?" I took the food from Colby.

"You wanna help me give her a quick bath before we eat? She'll be hungry soon, but we should have about twenty minutes."

"Yeah, no problem." I frowned. "Did you bring a baby bath?"

"Nah, we'll just use a towel and kinda sponge her down. It's not like she's covered in spit-up or had a huge blow-out. A quick bath is all she needs today."

We ended up using the bathroom sink and counter. Once she was all wiped down and lotioned up—smelling like the precious chunk of baby goodness she was—Colby made quick work of getting her into a diaper and pajamas.

He mixed up a bottle and fed her while I ate, then we switched, and I burped her while Colby wolfed down his food.

"You wanna take a walk? She usually settles pretty quickly when I walk or rock her." Colby glanced at his watch. "I think she's kinda off-schedule, but she should go down for the night and only wake twice if we're lucky."

So, we ended up walking the sidewalks of some Arizona town as a warm breeze blew and a full moon peeked over the horizon.

"It feels weird not holding her," Colby mused as we walked.

I didn't want to hand Elsie over, but I offered.

"No, she's comfy and you're doing a great job." He stretched his arms and sighed. "Didn't realize how much I was doing on my own until I had an extra set of hands to help." Glancing down at his daughter's sleepy eyes as we walked and I cradled her close, Colby went on, "Don't get me wrong, I'm not complaining. She wasn't planned, but I wouldn't trade her for the world. Just nice to have someone jump in—someone I can trust."

"It's crazy watching you be this amazing dad. I'd never really pictured you as a parent, but you make it look easy."

Colby scoffed. "It's the farthest thing from easy I've ever experienced. But she's worth it. The mess with Sasha was…well, a mess. But I'm grateful for what came of it."

"Can I say that I hate Sasha for leaving her baby, but I'm also glad she gave her up so Elsie wouldn't grow up weighed down by all of her mother's struggles?" Guilt raced through me, and I worried Colby would be angry at my truth.

"You and me both, man," he said with a long sigh. "She and I weren't meant to be—we would have parted ways eventually. But part of me screams a child should have their mother while the other part of me reminds me what it was like for me having my mother around. I don't want my kid suffering as she thinks about her mom leaving her or wonders why she wasn't enough for Sasha to stay, but I also don't want her suffering with an addict for a mother and wondering every single day why she's not good enough for her mom to pick her own kid over drugs." A pinched, far-away look etched Colby's face and I knew he was thinking of his childhood.

"If I have anything to say about it, this baby will never know life without the complete love and support of her entire family."

Colby smiled. "When I first knew we were pregnant, I freaked out because I knew there was no way I could do this by myself." He threw an arm around my shoulders. "But now, getting through those first few months, and knowing I've got all of you on my side, I know it will be hard, but I'm not as scared as I was back then."

Elsie finally gave in to sleep as we made our way back to the hotel. Colby moved the pack-n-play next to his side of the bed and turned off the lamp.

"I know she's not supposed to have anything in the bed with her, but I hate the thought of putting her in there with no blanket or pillow or anything."

Colby chuckled. "I know. But that's why she's in that warm sleeper and the sleep sack. And the air conditioning unit is on your side, she'll be warm enough. You've read the book." He gave me a wink.

"I know, I know. Nothing in bed with the baby. Still… can't imagine just lying there with no pillow or blanket."

"That's because you like to burrow under your pillow and hog all the blankets."

No lies detected.

I stood there a moment longer before finally giving Colby a desperate look.

"What?"

"I don't know how to lay her down. What if she wakes up?"

He shook his head with a smirk. "She'll be fine. She might wake a bit, but I doubt it. I'll take her and put her down if you want."

Nodding, I let Colby move Elsie from my arms to the pack-n-play. She sniffled and moved around but didn't wake.

"Now what?" I asked, feeling as if I'd helped disarm a bomb.

"Well, we could watch TV, but driving wore me out. She'll be up in about four hours, so I'm thinking sleep."

It wasn't late, but driving all day was exhausting. Knowing a tiny baby would be crying for a bottle and new diaper in just a few hours had me stressed and thinking sleep sounded like the best thing ever.

So, I brushed my teeth and shucked down to my boxer briefs before turning off the lamp. Colby made his way to the bathroom. A few minutes later, he rummaged through the diaper bag and then placed something on the dresser.

Pushing up on my elbows, I saw he'd put out all the makings for a bottle. In the shadowy darkness, I watched him toss a diaper, wipes, and rash cream on the bedside table before pushing his pants down and tossing them on the chair. In the same brand of boxer briefs I wore—we'd been wearing the same brand ever since freshman year when my mom took us shopping for school clothes and we decided this brand was the very best—Colby climbed into bed and turned on his side.

We wrestled with the blankets for a bit, but finally chuckled and settled in to sleep.

I knew Elsie would wake us up.

I knew Colby was my best friend *only* and any thought of him being more than that needed to stay deeply buried in my heart.

I knew we had a long drive the next day.

But for the time being, I was in bed with Colby—close enough to feel his warmth—and all was right with my world again.

CHAPTER 4

COLBY

Kai sat bolt-right up in bed when Elsie wailed for her first overnight bottle.

"Jesus," he gasped. "How does that not give you a heart attack every night?"

I chuckled sleepily and dragged myself out of bed. Reaching for my squalling baby, I gave her kisses and set to work getting her diaper changed.

"Oh my god," Kai groaned. "Feed her. She's breaking my heart." He rushed to the dresser and started mixing the bottle.

"You don't have to get up. I'll make this as quick as I can," I said as I put the dry diaper on my daughter. "It's best to change her first so I don't have to wake her up after her bottle. She usually goes back down quickly."

"I can help." Kai stood next to me and shook up the bottle. "Let me feed her."

My heart couldn't handle this man and how much he loved my baby.

I took the bottle from him, let him pick up the screaming baby, and helped him get situated in the chair to feed her.

Kai had absolutely no experience with babies, but his instincts with my daughter were on point, and I trusted him without question. I made a quick trip to the bathroom while he hummed a song as Elsie drained her bottle.

Taking the empty bottle from him, I whispered, "I can burp her."

He nodded and let me take her from him. By the time he'd used the restroom and gotten a drink, Elsie had burped, and I'd put her back down.

"We need to get into a routine where we're not both up for that," Kai said as we settled back into bed. "I can do the next one if you want to sleep."

"I won't sleep through her crying." I fixed my pillow and got comfortable. "Don't worry about getting up for the next one. I've got it."

Stubborn ass that he was, Kai rolled from bed when Elsie woke again. He mixed her bottle while I changed her diaper. Luckily, she went back down without a fuss once her belly was full, and we got a couple more hours of sleep.

She hadn't made a peep yet when I stirred in the morning, but something had woken me.

Heat.

And a scent I'd recognize anywhere.

Fuck.

I'd wrapped Kai in my arms, his back against my chest, my leg thrown over his.

Oh god.

So warm and solid.

He smelled so damn good.

My cock ached to press against him.

My lips begged to taste his skin.

And my heart nearly pounded out of my chest.

Holding Kai in my arms felt so right.

We'd be so good together—I wasn't sure *how* that knowledge had sprouted in my head, but I knew it without a shadow of a doubt.

But if he'd ever wanted anything with me, he would have told me. And it was ridiculous to think that just because my best friend was bi, he'd automatically be into me. I wasn't about to make a fool of myself by exposing my unrequited love.

Luckily, Elsie picked the right moment to save her daddy from an awkward moment and squawked her discomfort.

Rolling quickly out of bed, I yanked on my sweats in hopes of covering my morning wood, grabbed Elsie up, and started changing her diaper. Maybe if I stayed bent over for a while, things downstairs would ease up and save me from mortification.

Kai snuggled deeper into the blankets with a moan, but a few moments later, he got up and made his way to the bathroom. When he came back, he mixed up a bottle and ran a hand over his sleepy eyes. With any luck, he hadn't even realized I had him tucked into my arms when I woke up.

"You good if I go run?"

I nodded. "Yeah. You wanna get breakfast or grab something farther down the road?"

"Let's just get coffee here and we can eat later. I won't be hungry for a while."

So, I fed Elsie, showered while she played, and waited for Kai to finish his run and shower before we packed up and headed out.

The next three days were a blur of long drives, hotels, laughing with Kai, taking care of Elsie, and falling head-over-heels in love with my best friend.

By the time we were thirty minutes away from Peppermint Hollow, I'd resigned myself to the fact I'd likely go insane with the feelings I had for Kai. But everything would be worth it to be raising my baby at home with family.

Summer hadn't completely given up in the Midwest yet and the early fall day was overly warm for the time of year. At least we hadn't come from California straight into a Peppermint Hollow winter. After years in Florida and California, I'd need some time to adjust to the cold.

Hell, I needed a winter coat and Elsie needed warmer sleepers and bigger blankets. I'd kept her mostly in onesies and little shorts on the West Coast, but I saw long sleeves and long pants in her future as we headed into fall and winter.

"Whatcha thinkin'?" Kai asked as he glanced in the mirror to check on Elsie again.

"Just that we need warmer clothes," I mused.

Kai laughed, pointing at the temperature reading on the truck. "It's hot as balls for this time of year."

I chuckled. "Yeah, I know. But we both know it could be spitting snow within two days."

"Okay, you haven't forgotten how weather works in the Midwest, that's good."

I pulled the truck into Kai's driveway and looked at the house that was as much my home as the one next door had been. The homes on this street were old, beautiful, and full of charm. Kai's home sat next to the wide driveway; the garage located diagonally from the back door.

The house looked almost identical to the one I lived in so many years ago. Two-story, a mix of light and dark blonde brick, and dark wood. The large picture window made for Christmas-card-perfect photos during the holidays when a large tree shone cheerfully through the glass. The tall, thin window closer to the driveway caught attention due to its decorative arched design at the top.

With no front porch, only an ornate door with a small overhang, the house had a beautiful, large front yard. A well-kept sidewalk led from the door to the street; a brick-lined path veering from the bottom step to the driveway.

Three large trees flanked the home and provided shade and beauty all year round. The two maples put on a show in the fall and were already gearing up for their colorful splendor. The balsam fir had always been the most picture-perfect Christmas tree in my mind. When harsh, cold, icy weather descended on Peppermint Hollow, the evergreen stood tall and proud, its branches basking in the wind and snow.

Out of sight due to where I'd stopped the truck, the back of the house boasted a gorgeous patio area. Wooden table and chairs, loungers, and a firepit surrounded by Adirondacks invited friends and family to sit, relax, and stay for a while under the twinkly lights hung from the rafters under the tin roof.

The backyard was small compared to the front, but the

patio reduced mowing time and made the area all the more welcoming. Eric and Lacy, Kai's parents, had kept the place immaculate and I expected Kai would do the same.

Cataloging the house had been a decent distraction, but all too soon, my head brought me back to the present. Trying to breathe through the tightness in my chest, I reminded myself that coming home was my choice and it was for the best. Everyone would be arriving soon—we'd given them our approximate time of arrival with a slight cushion for travel delays—but I needed a moment to just wrap my head around the fact I was back in Peppermint Hollow.

My demons might have still been rattling around in my head, but my mother was gone. My dad and I were good. The Jacksons were as much family to me as my father and Allison—if not more thanks to our history. And Kai was by my side.

Everything was right in my world.

Elsie, home, job, friends, family. I truly wanted for nothing.

Except for how badly you want down your best friend's pants. How's that gonna work when he goes out or brings a date home?

Fuck.

"Hey, talk to me. What's up?"

I shook my head. "Just not sure how I fucked so much up and still ended up with all of this."

Kai gripped my forearm. "You haven't fucked anything up—no more so than any of us fuck things up."

I scoffed. "I don't deserve all of this." I gestured vaguely toward the house, but I meant Kai standing by me, my family, a great job, a baby I'd die for in a heartbeat.

He sighed. "I know you've got a lot of shit to deal with, but I need you to believe me when I say there's no one better to be Elsie's dad, and you deserve every good thing that comes your way."

My eyes stung and I shook my head, glancing out the window at the very first hints of color dancing between leaves as the warm breeze blew through the trees. The house next door—the one I grew up in—had a decorative fall flag, amazing mums, and a fall wreath on the door. I didn't miss the colorful little LGBTQIA+ sticker on the corner of the front door window.

Kai had been my biggest supporter and cheerleader from the time we were five. Of course, he'd say I deserved everything good. But when you grew up with a parent who always picked a high over you, it was hard to think you were worthy of anything, let alone the good stuff.

"Who bought the house?" I nodded toward my old home.

"Haven't met him yet. His name is Blake. Your dad said he's nice. Physical therapist, I think. He's attractive." Kai waggled his brows before he threw open the truck door, letting in a giant blast of warm air.

Oh god. Did Kai have a thing for the new neighbor guy? The man living in my old house hooking up with Kai while I lived in my best friend's house...fuck, if that didn't scream of messy.

But Kai went on. "It's been weird being back *in* town after living on the outskirts for so many years."

"You like it?"

He shrugged. "Yeah. Supposedly good neighbor next

door." He threw a thumb over his shoulder. "The two guys who live over there are life-long townies, but they haven't lived there long."

I glanced toward the old house we'd always called the Christmas House when we were kids. "Wait, so the physical therapist has a rainbow sticker. You're bi. And there are two guys living in that house? Is this like the queer corner of town now?"

Kai laughed. "First, I have a sticker too. The town council handed them out to anyone who wanted one; more a sign of support than anything. Second, I hadn't even thought about it. Sure you want to move in here? Don't want to mess with your het vibe," he teased.

I tensed. "You know that shit doesn't bother me." *If I wasn't so chicken shit, you'd know just how much it doesn't bother me.*

Kai slapped my leg. "Just givin' you shit, man. The two guys over there are definitely together."

"Do we know them?"

"I recognize the one who's around our age. Don't think we ran in the same circles in high school. The younger one I don't recognize." He waggled his brows. "Pretty sure there's something going on between these two." He gestured between the Christmas House across the side street and my old house.

"Like what?"

"Well, I'm pretty sure the guy who visits the Christmas House a lot—friend or brother if I've clocked him right—is sneaking around with Blake the physical therapist."

I shook my head. "You always were a shit-stirrer. What makes you think that?"

Kai threw up his hands. "Look, I'm just saying, I haven't met any of them yet. Haven't been here more than a day or two without moving or tons of work to do. But he's comfortable with the guys over there." He tilted his head to the Christmas House where I saw a bright sign on the garage touting *Ivy's Auto*. "He sneaks in the back door or side door over here." He climbed out of the truck. "Don't worry, I'll get to the bottom of it. Even Francis has noticed."

"Francis?" My eyes immediately went to the house behind Blake's. "Oh my god, I haven't thought of Francis in years. He was so old…"

"Ha! We *thought* he was old. He was probably only like fifty-something. I think he's closing in on eighty now."

"He still spy on everyone in town and keep the grapevine in business?"

"From what my parents said, definitely. But he's harmless and I always remember he was kind." Kai glanced at his house. "I think we need to have an open house type thing. Invite the neighbors so we can meet everyone."

"You just want to try to figure out the mystery." I opened my door and stood, groaning as I stretched my legs.

"Yeah, so?" Kai got out and mimicked my stretch.

We got Elsie, the luggage, and headed inside.

The inside of the house was exactly as I remembered it, just missing some of the furniture Eric and Lacy had taken or Kai had gotten rid of. Inside the front door, a little foyer area led to four direction options.

Off to the right was the kitchen. The cabinets had been replaced when we were in high school, the counters and backsplash a neutral tile, the appliances black and stainless steel, and the floor a marbled tile.

From a brief glance, it appeared Kai hadn't kept the table and chairs. Which meant the one I brought with me would be absolutely perfect.

The kitchen led to the dining room which looked out the large picture window into the front yard.

To the left of the foyer was the living room with the tall decorative window trimmed in stained glass. Kai's recliner sat in a corner and a large, flatscreen TV hung on the wall. The hardwood floors gleamed, and I recalled the summer Lacy had hired a crew to remove the carpet in that room; Kai and I had spent hours in our socks running and sliding across the new, shiny wood once the floors had been sanded and waxed.

Back in the foyer, I looked slightly to the right of the stairs and saw the hall bathroom, a door that opened to the basement stairs, the laundry room, and the ninety-degree turn that led to the main bedroom and its bathroom. Off the laundry room was a small back porch area that looked out onto the patio.

Glancing up the stairway, I recalled the two bedrooms on the second floor and their shared bathroom, the large storage closet, and the den-type area where Kai and I played hours and hours of video games.

"Same as you remember?" Kai asked.

"Like I never left."

I gave Elsie a bottle while Kai carried things in from the truck. Then we switched and he changed her diaper while I walked in and out of the late summer heat with my arms full.

"Colby!" Kai yelled as I put a box down in the kitchen.

My heart sank and I bolted to the living room where Kai had Elsie on a blanket for a diaper change. "What?" I asked, skidding to a halt.

He beamed up at me as Elsie kicked her legs and cooed. "She smiled. At me. It wasn't gas, I swear. She smiled at me."

Elsie chose that moment to make a gurgling noise and churn her little legs, a gummy grin lighting up her face.

"See," Kai exclaimed. "That's a smile and it was for me. She can't even see you way over there."

I chuckled. "I told you she likes you, she just needed some time to get used to having you around. Now you're her best buddy."

We sat, shoulders pressed together, while Elsie made precious little baby sounds. "Better get her diaper on, I don't want to risk her peeing all over the place." Kai made quick work of the diaper and got the onesie back into place just as a knock sounded at the door.

Assuming it was our parents, I left Kai with the baby and went to let them in. Instead of finding the Jacksons or my dad and Allison, I was greeted by a smiling man in glasses and a dark-haired, tattooed man.

"Hi, we're Ivy and Emory. We live across the street." The guy in the glasses gestured to the Christmas House which stood across the side street to the left. "We've been sucky neighbors and figured it was beyond time to come introduce ourselves. Thought we could offer help carrying the heavy stuff in too."

I recognized the guy with the ink. We'd definitely gone to school together, but Kai was right in saying we didn't run in the same circles. I remembered him having a friend

—kinda an odd couple type thing—but other than that, I knew very little about the man.

Stepping back, I let them in. "Come on in. I'm Colby Burke." I held out my hand to shake.

"Ivy Gregory," the dark-haired guy said. "I own Ivy's Auto. Happy to service your vehicles at a good price if you're in the market."

"For sure. Just moved here from California, I'll need a mechanic."

"Emory Bell." The guy with glasses and great smile shook my hand. "I help Ivy at the shop."

At that moment, Kai walked to the door with Elsie cradled in his arms and I worried my heart would ooze to the ground in a gooey mess.

"Hi, I'm Kai Jackson," he said, holding out his free hand to shake. "I've been a shit new neighbor by not coming over to say hi."

"Oh my god," Emory gushed just as Ivy said, "No worries."

"You have the most gorgeous baby," Emory continued.

Kai beamed, not even blinking at the assumption Elsie was his. *Ours*. "Thanks. This is Elsie Mae. You met her dad. They're moving in."

Voices coming up the front porch stairs interrupted, and greetings and hugs were shared all around.

Over the next little bit of time, Allison and Lacy took turns gushing over and holding Elsie while Eric, Dad, Kai, Ivy, Emory, and I got the recliner, the table and chairs, and the miscellaneous items moved from the U-Haul into the house.

We also worked out a few six-degrees of separation shit.

Emory and Ivy had been on a television show last year which was partially why they looked familiar. I hadn't watched it, but I remembered the commercials.

"The Season's Streaming channel is supposed to replay Once Upon a Christmas House this season, so we'll let you watch it to see how we did," Emory said with a smile. "I won't be responsible for spoilers."

Emory had worked at the Peppermint Café upon returning from college which was why our families recognized him. He and Ivy had lived in Peppermint Hollow all their lives. Dad and Eric took their cars to Ivy's Auto. It was one of those situations where most of the parties involved knew of each other but hadn't been more than just a vague acquaintance.

"You guys probably went to school together," Emory said.

Ivy snorted. "I wasn't exactly in the popular crowd."

"Trevor was." Emory glanced at me. "My brother. He and Ivy are like best friends."

I nodded. "I remember them."

Kai made a noise of recognition. "Yeah, I do too. Trevor was super smart—he was in a few of my classes. You guys were definitely a...different...mixture."

Ivy smirked. "You could say that."

"I missed the show last year, but I want to watch it when they replay it," Kai said. "Didn't I hear something about your brother was going to be on the show first?"

Emory winced. "It's like one of the worst-kept secrets in town. Trevor got in a wreck right before filming was set to start. They let me replace him."

Kai's eyes went wide. "And you two ended up together?"

Ivy put his arm around Emory and the younger man grinned. "Yep. And Trevor ended up with—" He yelped when Ivy poked him.

"No, Little Bell. That's not your story," Ivy warned.

Emory huffed. "Fine."

"Your brother is around here a lot, right?" Kai asked with a gleam in his eyes.

"Yeah, he visits us a lot," Emory said. "He doesn't live far, and he knows others around here, one in partic—"

Ivy clapped a hand over Emory's mouth.

Kai smiled wickedly and I knew if Emory and Kai got together, the secrets would spill in a heartbeat.

So, we all kinda knew each other, but we were pretty much strangers. I had a feeling if Kai and Emory had any say in things, we'd be spending a lot of time with our neighbors.

And Kai was likely already planning a way to get to the bottom of the Trevor and Blake story, with help from Emory.

Dad and Eric volunteered to return the U-Haul.

Allison and Lacy were enthralled with their new granddaughter.

Emory and Ivy said goodbye with the promise we'd get together for dinner soon.

"Come with me," Kai said.

I eyed Elsie, but she was sound asleep in Allison's arms, so I followed Kai to the kitchen. He handed me a beer and headed outside to the patio.

"It's so weird to think of living here as adults," I muttered. "But it also feels like we never left."

"Yeah, like I'm in charge of the yard and the appliances and shit now. Mom and Dad won't be taking care of things." Kai cracked open his beer. "But it feels like yesterday that we had a million campouts and gashed our knobby knees open on the concrete."

We settled in the patio chairs and sipped our beers. The warm breeze held the promise of fall, and I breathed in deeply, trying to relax. "Do you think I need to get a babysitter for Elsie?"

Kai cocked his head. "Hadn't given it much thought. With both of us here, we can probably split it, but it may not be fair to her if we're not completely present." He pointed his beer bottle my way. "Pretty sure Mom and Allison would gladly volunteer to watch her. If they both took one day a week, that would leave us with just two main days, since Friday is light anyway."

"Don't want to assume anything," I hedged.

He chuckled. "You saw them in there, right? Mom has a flexible schedule at the community center, and Allison makes her own hours at the salon. I'm one hundred percent positive they'll gladly each give a day to watching their granddaughter. And how lucky is Elsie to have two sets of grandparents in her life?"

A brief flicker of guilt sparked in me.

Sasha's parents.

I'd never met them. Did they know about Elsie? Would they be the types to want to be part of her life? Sasha claimed they weren't great when she was growing up and she wanted nothing to do with them during our time together.

I smiled, warmth filling my chest at how easily Kai and his parents had accepted me into their lives way back then, and how they did it again without even a moment's hesitation now when I brought my daughter home. "Yeah, we can see if they'd want to. We'll see if we can handle the other days. If not, we can see about a sitter."

The buzz of the beer and the soft breeze lulled my drive-tired ass into a light doze, but for the first time in a long time, things felt right. Not perfect, but right.

Like coming home was the beginning of something big.

CHAPTER 5

KAI

"NICE AFTERNOON." A VOICE STARTLED BOTH OF us from our dozing on the patio.

Nearly knocking over my beer, I jerked to a more upright position just as Colby grunted awake beside me.

Francis Sullivan leaned against the back fence and gave a little wave with his friendly, old-man smile. "Didn't mean to scare you. Just taking Miss Priss for a walk and thought I'd say hello." He ran his hand over the head of his feline companion. The cat was decked out in a pink diamond collar and a matching halter leash.

I knew Colby was dying to ask if the cat was the same one from back when we were kids, and I willed him not to open his mouth. Poor Francis had been reduced to tears a few weeks ago when he reminisced about his first and second Miss Prisses from so many years ago.

Colby, flipping on the charm, stood and made his way to the fence. "Mr. Sullivan, it's great to see you again."

Francis squinted his eyes and studied Colby. "Well, I'll be. I thought you were just a friend of Kai's come to visit.

But it's Colby Burke as I live and breathe. Son, I haven't seen you in years. Are you here to see your dad?"

Colby's cheeks pinked deliciously. "Nah, decided it was time to come home for good. This one," he nodded toward me, "said we could stay with him for a bit."

You can stay with me forever if I have my way.

"You brought your wife?" Francis asked, always in others' business.

Colby cleared his throat. "Um, no. No wife. Just me and my baby."

I thought Francis's brow might shoot up so far it would forever be lost in his comb-over.

"Baby? No wife?" Francis tutted. "I'll have to come over for tea some afternoon and hear that delectable story." The cat squirmed in his arms as if to express her opinion that today *not* be that day. "Without Miss Priss, of course. She can only tolerate the outdoors for short periods of time. She's very sensitive."

I joined them at the fence. "Come on over when you see us out."

Francis eyed the two of us, back and forth, definite opinions and questions forming. But he just nodded. "I'll do that. Have to say, it does an old man's heart good to see the two of you back together. You were thick as thieves way back then."

"Never really stopped," Colby said. "Kai can't go a day without talking to me." He bumped me with his shoulder.

"Whatever." I elbowed him. "Colby missed small-town living so much, he begged me to bring him home."

Giving Colby shit—and him dishing it my way—made my heart happy. We hadn't missed a day of talking to each other since we were five, even if it was just quick texts during our busiest, most hectic times, but having him right beside me hit differently.

Francis grinned. "Ah, yes. I see everything is right in the world now that CoJack has reunited. You two always were the quintessential peas in a pod. I'm happy for you; may all your hopes and wishes come true." He gave a wink. "Christmas is coming, and we all know just how well the holiday magic works in these parts."

He put Miss Priss down, allowing her to stretch before she pranced through the grass toward the house behind mine, Francis shuffling behind her.

"What the hell is he on about?" Colby muttered.

"You know the rumors around town, about the Christmas magic." I shrugged. "Just an old man entertaining himself."

Colby grunted.

"But you *do* need to get rid of your flair for getting Scrooge-y around the holidays," I said, poking him in the arm. "We've got a baby now and she's gonna grow up thinking Christmas in a small town is the best damn thing in the entire world."

Colby froze, his eyes boring into mine. For a split second, I thought he was angry, but then a soft smile lit up his face. "*We've* got a baby, huh?"

My cheeks heated, but I didn't care. "I mean, I don't think it's such a stretch for me to love my best friend's baby like my own," I mumbled.

He shook his head. "It's appreciated. All of this...it means more than you know. When I left—"

The back door opened and Dad stepped out. "Return is all taken care of. Final receipt is being emailed."

The rest of the day and into the evening was spent

with the grandparents doting over Elsie Mae, and all of us chatting and hanging out like an evening together was something we'd been doing our whole lives.

I watched Colby glow as we all loved on his baby. Watched him bask in easy conversation with his dad— something that had been sorely missing during his childhood. And I kicked myself for not demanding he return home years ago. He *needed* this, needed his family.

Huffing a sigh, I admitted that bringing him home years ago would have been a disaster. He wasn't ready; he would have fought tooth and nail, and I may have lost my best friend. And if he'd come home back then, he wouldn't have Elsie now. I knew he'd been shocked and terrified of becoming a father—and even more so to being a single father—but I also knew having a baby had changed Colby in a way he'd never seen coming.

And despite longing for him to be back home for all those years, this was one of those instances where the timing was just right. Colby was home *now* because life had a funny way of working out in mysterious and perfect ways.

☙❧

"I'm so excited about Christmas," Emory squealed as he poured more candy in the bucket about a month later.

Colby, Elsie, and I had settled into our new cohabitation with the ease of two guys who had known each other their whole lives and were learning the ways of being a parent.

Colby hadn't batted an eyelash when I'd indicated we'd share my big bed and keep Elsie in her little bed in our room. If he'd realized he had me all tangled in his arms every morning on our road trip, he didn't act like it. And it was getting harder and harder to pretend like we didn't wake up all octopused together ever since he'd moved in. He *had* to know, right? We'd always been physical with each other. We were exhausted from work and parenting. Waking up in his arms was very much what I wanted to do every single day, but it was also the worst and best torture ever.

But if Colby didn't mention it or act like it was an issue, I wasn't going to ruin what we had. Even if it probably wasn't purposeful on his part.

We were asleep.

Neither of us were dating or getting any action other than our right hands.

It made sense that two tired, touch-starved guys would gravitate toward each other during the night.

That was my story, and I was sticking to it.

Glancing at Colby on our first Halloween together in several years, I couldn't help the way my heartbeat increased. Was I a complete fool? Yeah, probably. But it was better to live with the deep ache in my heart for my best friend than to try to live without him by my side.

The Halloween night was typical for October in the Midwest. Why did the holiday always have to turn out cold and wet? We'd opted to hang with Emory and Ivy, and their dog Magic, at the auto shop since the garage was heated. Kids who stopped for treats loved the decorations Emory had insisted on putting up, and their parents appreciated the ten percent off coupons Ivy handed out.

Magic, a gorgeous Black Lab—full name: Christmas Magic—had taken to Elsie like a guard dog from the first moment we let him sniff her. He was always near whoever was holding the baby and watched her with sharp, lovey-dovey eyes. This time next year, Elsie and Magic would be inseparable. At least, that's what the dog was longing for, I could tell.

I had Elsie strapped to me in the baby wrap, and we all enjoyed mulled wine, smiling at the little ones who braved the cold to show off their costumes and collect sweets. The baby wrap—really, just a simple piece of cloth with a couple metal loops...and some didn't even have the hardware—had been a lifesaver over the last month.

I'd watched several videos about baby-wearing and built on the little bit I'd learned when I first bought the wrap. Colby and I took turns wearing Elsie around on days when Allison or Mom didn't have her. Keelie, our godsend babysitter, came for about four hours each day our parents couldn't watch Elsie. The schedule seemed to be working for everyone, and our business had actually grown since Colby came home, but having the baby wrap had proved to be a blessing. We agreed Elsie would get her tummy time and playtime, but wearing her close to our chests felt right for the time being.

The thought of next year's Halloween had my heart all aflutter. Would Colby still live with me? Would we take a dressed-up Elsie around the neighborhood with Magic by her side? Or would he have moved on and want to spend the evening with his new girlfriend?

Pulling myself from the sobering thoughts, I absorbed what Emory had said. "Christmas? Don't you even want to give a moment of thought to Thanksgiving?"

Ivy grunted. "Em's veins pump red and green. He'd celebrate all year if we let him."

"Thanksgiving is crap. I love the whole idea of being thankful and gathering with friends and family, but I'm not about continuing—or even starting—a tradition based on the annihilation of a whole group of people." Emory shook the bucket of candy, grabbed a piece of chocolate, and returned the treats to the little table where tiny grabby hands could easily reach. Magic lifted his head as if to check for any dropped goodies, but huffed and went back to dozing, keeping his ear on any peeps Elsie might make.

"Fair point," I said.

"You guys decorate for Christmas?" Colby asked. "I remember being in awe of the house as a kid."

Ivy huffed but threw an arm around Emory's shoulders and nuzzled his boyfriend's cheek. "If I had my way, no. But Emory's a spoiled brat who somehow gets his way, so yes, we decorate."

Emory's cheeks pinked. "I do the inside—I like to include some of the vintage items that were left in the attic when Ivy moved in."

"And by vintage, what he really means is The Creeps."

Emory rolled his eyes. "Ivy nicknamed some of the older, more unique pieces The Creeps because he's—"

"Swear to god, Em," Ivy warned, love and fun in his voice. "You know damn well those things are creepy as hell. The Santa and Nutcracker are the worst."

Emory just laughed. "We hired someone to do the outside last year and it's totally the way to go."

"We'll decorate inside for sure this year. I want to see Elsie in awe of the pretty lights on the tree." I kissed the top of her sleeping head. "Not sure on the outside, depends on what Dad has in the garage." I wrinkled my brow. "Come to think of it, I don't remember seeing the Christmas decorations when I was moving shit in. Mom may have tossed everything."

"We can make a weekend of it," Emory offered. "I'll help you, you help me, while the Scrooges grunt and groan."

Ivy started to protest, but Emory shrugged as he smiled sweetly at his boyfriend. "Or you can go Black Friday shopping with me. We could make a whole day of it. Up before the sun, spend the entire day at the mall and shops. Not fall into bed until late that night."

Colby shot Ivy an amused look and the tattooed man pretended to shudder. "You and Kai have a blast with the decorating, Em. I'll be in the garage. All. Day. Maybe all weekend."

"Hey," Emory's brother, Trevor, said as he walked into the garage and ladled himself some mulled wine. Magic jumped up to inspect the new arrival and sniff him up and down, likely smelling Trevor's two dogs on him. "Had a lot of kids come by?" The man was the typical boy-next-door. Very attractive, successful, and I knew from high school, really smart. But I also recognized someone who was flushed and flustered when I saw it.

So did his little brother, and he swooped in with gusto.

"Why are you so…" Emory gestured vaguely toward Trevor.

"What?" Trevor asked, gulping more wine. "I'm not."

Emory's big brown eyes narrowed behind his glasses. "You *are*. Your cheeks are pink and you're all…ruffled."

"I'm not ruffled."

"Leave the man alone, Em," Ivy said, grabbing his boyfriend around the waist and pulling him to sit on his lap. For a moment, his best friend looked relieved by the save. "Trevor is a big boy. When he wants to tell us about the secret he's keeping from us, he will."

Trevor's wide eyes landed on his best friend. "I'm not…" He swallowed and finished off his wine. "Um, just wanted to stop by and say hey."

Emory squirmed on Ivy's lap. "Just in the area and wanted to see us, huh?"

"Yeah," Trevor answered absently. "We still doing the Friendsgiving thing?"

"Yep. You'll be there?" Emory asked.

"Yeah." Trevor ran a hand through his hair. "Can I bring a friend?"

"You know you can. Maybe actually bring this one? Last Christmas you were supposed to bring a friend and ended up coming alone."

"That was…this is different."

"You're always welcome to bring anyone you want," Ivy said, his eyes catching his friend's and communicating something meant just for Trevor. They reminded me of the friendship Colby and I had.

Even though my heart begged for what Colby and I had to be *more*.

CHAPTER 6

COLBY

AFTER READING A CHAPTER IN OUR BOOK *and* reading articles online, Kai and I decided we liked what one article said about introducing solids before six months. "Pediatricians say not until six months, but there's also emerging evidence that introducing solids around four months old may make baby more likely to eat fruits and veggies later in life and may decrease risk of food allergies. So, maybe see what your doc thinks. It's suggested to add an iron-fortified cereal mixed with formula or breast milk for a week or so. If baby does well with that, mix in some fruits or veggies. Another suggestion is to start with veggies since babies usually like the fruits better. Remember, only one new food at a time so you know the culprit if there's a rash or reaction."

Kai picked up Elsie with a huge grin on his face. "Guess what, Elsie Mae? You get some cereal for that sweet tummy." Elsie gave him her gummy smile and cooed. She was as in love with the man as I was—truly, the awe in her eyes when she saw Kai's face or heard his voice was adorable.

It made my heart hurt to think about how much we'd both miss the man when we had to move out.

Why would you have to move out?

I rolled my eyes at the stupid thought. Of course, we'd have to move out; we couldn't stay at Kai's forever. I knew we were cramping his style. True, Kai didn't date *a lot*, but he went out and occasionally had people he kept around for longer than a couple dates. Having a baby changed all that and it wasn't fair of me to think Kai would want to just put his whole life on hold.

Hell, maybe he wanted to meet up for beers with Blake from next door.

Or go on a date with the cousin Keelie kept trying to hook one of us up with.

"So, we'll add the cereal for dinner?" Kai asked, dancing Elsie around the room.

"Yeah, probably better this evening than at Ivy and Emory's place, just in case she hates it."

Friendsgiving was the next day, but I wanted Elsie's first taste of food to be with just Kai and me.

We went about the rest of our day. Keelie came by and took Elsie off our hands for a bit. Taking turns, Kai and I finished up work things for the long weekend and tidied up the house. He still hadn't furnished all the rooms, but we both had a neat streak when it came to keeping things organized—aside from Kai's tendency to toss his towel wherever after a shower.

The baby safety lady had come and shown us all the dangers—obvious and hidden—for when Elsie became mobile. We'd immediately taken care of everything, knowing once our girl was on the move, we likely wouldn't have time to do it sufficiently.

The fact that Kai had even thought of safety, let alone called in a specialist, still warmed my heart.

It turned out that adding cereal to Elsie's diet was a bit of a letdown. She seemed pretty neutral about the whole thing. She took bites, but there were no excited faces. No yuck faces. She ate it and that was pretty much it.

"Well, that was boring as hell, Else," Kai exclaimed as he wiped her face and hands. "Your dads lead a plain life; we need you to keep things exciting."

Kai froze just as my heart squeezed.

"Sorry, I—" he started.

"You're as much her dad as I am," I said, stepping close and brushing a kiss over my daughter's head. Wrapping an arm around his neck, I kissed his temple. Something I'd done maybe a million times. Pressing a kiss to his cheek—not unusual for us—I breathed him in deeply and scolded those parts of my head and heart shrieking at me to move to his lips. "We're both lucky to have you in our lives."

I pulled away and reached for Elsie, doing my best to ignore the fire burning in my belly and the curious look on Kai's face.

It would have been so easy to just kiss him and tell him how I felt.

But that wasn't what we were to each other.

If Kai felt that way toward me, he would have told me.

I needed to work my way through whatever this was and move on.

The way my heart thumped and begged for me to

reach out for him meant that would be easier said than done.

But I could do it.

If it meant keeping my best friend in my life, I could do anything.

❧

Having my lips on Kai's skin had set fire to something deep inside. I hated it and loved it. Maybe I was imagining the awkwardness between us. I had to be because nothing had really changed. I still longed to touch him, loved him like no other, and couldn't imagine my life without him.

We still woke up tangled in each other's arms and pretended it didn't happen.

Still went about our day taking care of Elsie and cracking jokes.

But I swore there was an undercurrent of...

Something.

On my side, I couldn't stop thinking about how that brief press of my lips to his cheek had tasted—a hint of salt, moisturizer, *Kai*. The bristle of his scruff under my lips. How good it would have been to capture his mouth and feast on him the way I'd longed to do for so long.

On Kai's side, he seemed...I don't know...I could have been making it all up...but he seemed...

Off.

And that was from a kiss to his cheek. Something we'd done for years.

Did I need to say something? But what? *Hey, I know I've kissed you on the cheek for most of our lives, and I didn't mean to make this one weird. But oh yeah, I'm in love with you and have been since long before I left Peppermint Hollow.*

No.

If Kai was upset, he'd talk to me.

I needed to get out of my head and stop making a big deal about something that was truly nothing.

Friendsgiving was a decent distraction.

Magic glued himself to whoever was holding Elsie as usual. Guests included Ivy, Emory, Trevor, Kai, and me for the first little bit. My dad and Allison had taken Eric and Lacy to a soup kitchen to volunteer for the day.

Kai kept throwing me looks or I'd look up and catch him watching me.

Or maybe that was my wishful thinking.

Emory eyed us suspiciously which only made me wonder if there really *was* something to me thinking things were off between Kai and me.

Luckily, a knock at the door had Trevor shooting out of the kitchen like his ass was on fire. "I'll get it."

Emory followed his big brother like the stealthy little elf he was, peeking around the door frame to watch as Trevor opened the door for the guest.

A gasp from Emory, followed by, "I *knew* it," brought the rest of us to the doorway to watch the goings-on.

Trevor sighed, his cheeks red, but he let himself be pulled close to the man at his side. Blake gave a sheepish little wave. "Hi, thanks for having me."

Before Ivy could grab him, Emory made his way toward Blake and Trevor. "I knew it. I knew something was going on between you two. How long were you going to keep it a secret if I hadn't seen you playing tonsil hockey at my front door?" He sounded somewhat hurt, but mostly ecstatic.

Trevor ran a hand through his hair. "Want to maybe sit and we'll fill you in? We planned on telling you today anyway."

Ivy wrapped an arm around Emory's neck and pulled his boyfriend's back flush to his front. "Probably would have gone better if *someone* hadn't been sneaking around and spying."

"It's *my* house and *my* brother," Emory said with a pout.

Grateful for the distraction from my own mixed-up feelings, I took a seat next to Kai for the storytelling. Things were possibly weird—or I was just overthinking everything —but there was no way to break the bonds we'd built over twenty-five years. No way I was sitting anywhere else. Plus, he had Elsie; I sat close to my daughter. And Magic, of course.

Once we were all seated, Trevor glanced at Blake and let him take his hand. "So, everyone, meet Blake." The smirk covered up his nervousness, but I could tell the guy was sweating bullets.

"Everyone knows Blake," Emory said. "What we don't know is the story behind why the two of you have been sneaking around behind our backs. Has this been going on since last Christmas?"

Trevor's head shot up. "What? No." He narrowed his eyes at his little brother. "Wait, how did you know we were sneaking around?"

Ivy chuckled and ran a hand over his scruffy chin. "First, you weren't very stealthy. Even I caught on and I'm usually pretty oblivious. Second, Emory is like a dog with a bone. Once he got the slightest sniff there was something between you two, he wasn't letting it go."

Trevor sighed. "No, we weren't together last year. I mean, I knew him, he was my physical therapist—"

"Was he the *someone special* you met at physical therapy? The one you were going to bring to dinner last year?" Emory asked.

Trevor shrugged. "I think, in my heart, I said that because I wished it would be Blake. I *did* go out with a girl I met there, but it was a total bust because I was already hung up on him."

Blake cleared his throat. "I was going through a shit divorce. I lived a couple towns over, the drive to work was terrible, my home life was a disaster. Plus, he was my patient; I couldn't get involved. No matter how badly I wanted to."

Emory made a fast-forward gesture. "Okay, so how did you get to this point?" He cocked his head. "And obviously I have no problem with it, but when did you start having a thing for guys?"

Trevor chuckled. "About the time this one started torturing me in physical therapy."

Ivy reached out to fist-pump his best friend. "Sneak-attack bi; I get it man. Everything is going along all smooth sailing and shit, and then *bam*."

My gut clenched. While I wouldn't say it was a surprise, I definitely hadn't been *planning* to fall for my best friend. But there had been a low-level burning ache in the depths of my soul for so many years, I couldn't even remember if it had taken me by surprise all those years ago. In some ways, my head and heart had loved Kai for so long, I couldn't remember a time when I wasn't neck-deep in everything I felt for him.

I brought my attention back to the story. Better to focus on someone else's drama than my own. At least until I nearly drove myself crazy with it all.

Trevor's cheeks flamed to life, and he bit his lip. From the bits of what I remembered of the man back in high school, he definitely wasn't used to being flustered. Blake had really thrown him for a loop.

Kinda like how Kai had thrown me for a loop.

And there went my gut again. Thinking about how my heart and body responded to having Kai close to me. Waking up with him wrapped in my arms. The scent of his soap and everything that made him Kai when I pressed my lips to his cheek. The way Elsie's eyes lit up for him and the fucking unbelievable way he'd taken to being her daddy.

Because that's what he was. No doubt in my mind. I didn't know if I'd ever be able to open up to him about how I felt, but I knew one hundred percent that we'd raise Elsie together. I wasn't counting on that in the beginning, but from the moment he took her in his arms, I knew we were in it together.

Even if he starts dating someone? Or if you lose your mind and try to get involved with someone again?

Focus.

I needed to focus on Trevor and Blake's story.

"He'd worked me over to near collapse one day," Trevor was saying.

Blake scoffed. "I made you do the exercises we'd agreed upon so you could get back to walking and running." He gripped Trevor's thigh. "Which you can do almost flawlessly now. You're welcome."

Trevor smirked. "Anyway, he had me in bad shape and I'd lost my damn mind. I kissed him."

"Then he proceeded to skip two therapy sessions. So, I took the liberty to just happen to be in the area and drive by his parents' house since he was staying there until he could do stairs again."

Trevor huffed out a sigh. "He waited until he saw me walk out to take a walk and ambushed me. Almost let it slip to Dad I'd missed a couple appointments and pretty much blackmailed me into getting into his car so I wouldn't miss that day's session."

Blake shrugged. "What? I'm dedicated to giving my clients what they need."

Emory snickered. "And what is it my big brother needed?"

Trevor shot him an exasperated look. "Blake is a professional and acted as if nothing happened. Never brought up the kiss. Meanwhile, over the next several sessions, I nearly drove myself insane wanting to kiss him again. But we started talking about his divorce and how messed up things were for him at home. I realized he wasn't in a position to act on what was maybe between us. So, I waited. Graduated physical therapy thanks to the best damn therapist in the world. Moved back to my apartment. And bided my time."

"We'd exchanged numbers at the end of therapy," Blake said. "The day my divorce was final, I texted him."

"We went out a few times—only outside of town; I wasn't ready to put a label on anything yet."

"Then I saw the house for sale," Blake explained. "I toured it, loved it, made an offer."

"And you two have been sneaking around ever since," Emory supplied. "Did you know Colby used to live there?"

Blake's brows shot up. "But you moved next door?"

"Kai and I were next door neighbors growing up. I left years ago. Dad and Allison sold the house and moved to the apartments—" I paused and nodded toward Trevor— "where you live if I'm not mistaken. Kai's parents moved to the retirement village. I moved back home and I'm staying with him for a while."

Kai coughed and I swear it sounded like he grumbled *bullshit*.

"It's a great house," Blake said.

I gave as much of a smile as I could muster. "It has potential with the right people. I hope that's you."

Blake gave a little nod and put his arm around Trevor. "Thanks. I hope it is too."

"So, are you two official? Dating? Boyfriends?" Emory asked.

"Damn, Em, let 'em breathe." Ivy took his boyfriend's hand.

Trevor swallowed thickly. "Official. Yeah. Boyfriends."

Emory whooped. "Thank god! No more sneaking around. It was driving me insane. You can just go in and out of his house like a damn normal person and not spend half your time trying to make sure I didn't know you'd just come from Blake's when you happened to show up at our door."

Trevor blushed again. "Yeah, I hear ya. I wasn't trying

to keep things from you. I just wasn't sure how to navigate everything."

"Well," Emory said, turning bright eyes toward Kai and me, "it looks like Colby's the only one not part of the LGBTQ+ community now." He batted his lashes. "Unless…"

Ivy cleared his throat and I swear he bit back a laugh.

My heart tried to claw its way out of my throat. I wasn't afraid to admit I was bisexual—or at the very least that I was into Kai—but I couldn't bear the thought of dropping that bomb on him and him rejecting me. He'd do it gently. Kai was always concerned about others. Knowing in your heart that your love is unrequited sucks balls; having your best friend—the object of that unrequited love—fumble through letting you down easy in front of people you were beginning to think of as friends would suck balls *and* fuck you sideways.

Kai put an arm around me and blew a slobbery kiss against my cheek. "He can be an honorary member until I wear him down."

I jerked away from the raspberry and wiped at my cheek as the guys laughed and stood.

Wait.

What?

Kai wanted to wear me down?

He was joking, right?

Fuck.

Now I had that little riddle planted in my mind to bug the shit out of me all night.

I took Elsie from Kai, trying not to decipher whatever that look was on his face.

Magic followed me to the kitchen where I mixed up a

bottle. The pup trailed me to the diaper bag where I made quick work of changing a soaking wet diaper. He then settled at my feet, eyes glued to Elsie's head while she fussed and flailed until I put the bottle to her lips.

The whole time, all I could think of was catching Kai alone and asking him what the hell he'd meant by that.

No. That was dumb. We joked all the time. Hell, we'd joked about getting together at thirty if we were both single. He'd made stupid comments about bringing me to the bi-side. I'd teased that he was the guy I'd go for if I ever went for guys.

But it was just joking.

Wasn't it?

Okay, maybe it wasn't joking for me. But Kai would have told me.

Right?

You've never told him.

God. We were fucking grown-ass men tiptoeing around a does-he-doesn't-he like-me situation like damn children. Maybe I should have just written him a note and asked him to circle yes or no.

I huffed out a frustrated breath.

Magic lifted his head and huffed back.

"Sorry," I mumbled. "She's fine. It's her daddy's head and heart that are all fucked up."

Magic eyed me for a bit before resting his chin on his paws and continuing to monitor the bottle drinking.

My heart swelled with pride as I watched my daughter's sleepy eyes. She already owned the hearts of two grown men and a dog. Add in the grandparents, the friends, and Keelie, and Elsie Mae had her very own fan club dedicated to loving and protecting her. Pretty impressive for a tiny human barely half a year old.

Once the bottle was finished and Elsie burped—to which Magic cocked his head in confusion—I placed her down for her nap. Her trusty protector cuddled next to the pack-n-play and looked at me as if daring me to tell him he couldn't be there.

I just patted Magic on the head and took the empty bottle to the kitchen.

"Ivy said come out to see the new hydraulic something he has in the shop," Emory said, gesturing toward Ivy's Auto.

Kai gave me a smirk over his wine glass. "Go on, you know you want to see the new toy."

Blake and Emory were discussing something about exercises for Ivy's lower back problems. I bit back a laugh when I thought of how Ivy would react to Emory telling people he had a bad back.

I made my way to the garage, the late November day cold but not freezing. Ivy offered me a beer and I clinked the bottle against his and Trevor's.

"The others didn't want to come out?" Ivy asked.

"Um, Kai was enjoying wine and always wants to be within earshot when Elsie is asleep," I said. "Blake and Emory were talking about exercises."

Ivy grunted. "I swear to god, Trev. If your little brother is telling your boyfriend about me throwing my back out—"

"No, no, no," Trevor chanted. "I may be thoroughly enjoying sex with a man these days, but I will *never* need to hear about my best friend and baby brother having sex."

Ivy slapped him on the back of the head. "I was going to say I threw my back out walking to the mailbox." He rolled his eyes. "It's embarrassing as hell. All I was doing was walking and then I couldn't move right for two days. But you're both my age, you'll deal with it soon enough." Then he gave an evil grin. "But a bad back gave me the perfect excuse to just lie back and let Em do all the dirty work for a few days."

"Fuck, man. Stop." Trevor ran a hand over his face. "Seriously. I know what Blake and I get up to, I do *not* want to think about you and Em."

Ivy laughed. "Fine, fine. It's just we have something new to bond over now."

Trevor cocked a brow. "We've been bonding most of our lives."

"Yeah, but now we both know we like dick—"

Ivy ducked the half-hearted shove Trevor attempted.

"How did you know?" I blurted.

Fuck.

Ivy and Trevor both stared at me, eyes wide and mischievous.

"Know what?" Ivy took a long swig of his beer.

I cleared my throat. "That you liked…" I gestured helplessly toward them as if I could make their words reappear.

"That we liked dick?" Ivy offered.

Choking on my beer, I forced the liquid down. "Dick. Guys. Specific guys." Oh god, my face burned, and I had no doubt my cheeks were blazing.

Trevor tossed his empty bottle in the trash. "Honestly, I didn't even give it a thought until Ivy fell for Emory during the show. Made me wonder how he'd never let on that he liked guys and girls both."

"Because I didn't ever really give it any thought either," Ivy interrupted. "I didn't really like anyone. Sex was sex. I wasn't looking for a relationship. When I started feeling shit for Emory, I let myself admit I found some guys attractive." He shrugged. "But for real, Emory's the only guy—only *person*—I've ever been willing to build something with."

Trevor nodded. "So, when he fell for Emory, I wondered if I could ever go for a guy. I mean, it's easy to see when someone is attractive. When I first started therapy, I was in a lot of pain. The first therapist I worked with just didn't mesh, so they switched me to Blake. If I hadn't already been reeling from the pain, I likely would have ended up on my ass. The man is hot and I dare anyone to deny that."

Ivy and I nodded. Blake was a good-looking guy, no doubt.

"But it wasn't until I got to know him that I really fell for him. I don't know why *he's* the one I got all gaga for when I've dated plenty, but I don't even question it. We work together and it is what it is," Trevor said.

"Any particular reason you're asking." Ivy drained the rest of his beer around a shit-eating grin.

"Just curious."

"Mmhm."

I glanced between the two best friends and knew I'd been had.

Giving it one last shot, I shrugged. "Yeah…"

"Wouldn't have to do with a lifelong best friend slash business partner slash roommate slash co-parent, would it?" Ivy asked, merriment bright in his eyes. How did a dark, broody, tattooed guy look so damn cheerful and pleased with himself?

Trevor slapped me on the back. "You don't have to tell us, but just know we understand what it's like being caught off guard falling for the person you least expect."

"What about when you fall for him as a teenager and spend the next decade running from shit in hopes you won't fuck up your friendship and lose him?" The words spilled out of me in a gush.

Ivy whistled.

Trevor gaped like a fish.

"Wait," Ivy said. "You've had a thing for Kai for over ten years and haven't told him?"

"Why?" Trevor asked.

"I'd rather have my best friend than mess it up by putting him in a bad position."

"Bad position?" Ivy asked. "Like under you? On top of you? Have you seen the way that man looks at you? I guarantee there is *no* position he'd consider bad as long as it's with you."

I shook my head. "No. Kai would have said something if he felt that way about me."

"Like you did?"

Closing my eyes, I breathed in deeply. "If he liked me the way I like him, I'd know."

"Is he just supposed to *know* how you feel?"

"No."

"Then why would you just know how he feels?" Trevor asked.

"Damn, Emory complains about angst and characters not communicating in the books he reads," Ivy said. "I think this is the real-life version of it. You two have never talked about this shit?"

"We talk. We've known each other since we were five." I crossed my arms over my chest. "We've joked around about getting together. But I'd never assume he likes me just because he's bi."

Ivy pinched the bridge of his nose. "And I bet Kai would never want to be the cliché bi guy falling for his straight best friend."

Trevor blew out a breath. "Damn, you two are a mess."

"We're fine," I argued. "As long as I don't ever let on—"

"No way," Ivy interrupted. "You can't keep doing that. It will eventually kill you. And I swear he has the same feelings for you. You guys need to *talk* about this shit. Stop dancing around the damn elephant in the room. Ten years? Fuck, man."

I glanced toward the house. "You really think he feels the same?"

"I'd put money on it," Ivy said. "But you never know unless you talk to him."

"And if I tell him how I feel, and he bolts?" The words sent fear coursing through me.

"You have a twenty-five-year friendship to fall back on," Trevor said.

"Or," I hedged. "I could just keep things the way they are. He's my best friend. I can't think about life without him."

"You could keep things the way they are. I don't see you getting involved with anyone else. Kai seems happy as a clam having you and Elsie by his side." Ivy nodded, his lips pursed. "So, you guys can go on with the status quo."

He gripped the back of my neck. "But think about all you'd miss out on. You've already missed over ten years."

His words punched me in the gut.

I stared at the house.

"Look, if I know Emory, he's in there grilling Kai and urging him to tell you how he really feels," Ivy said.

Trevor nodded. "Blake barely knows you guys, but he thought you two were together. He was shocked to find out you were just friends." He chuckled. "In fact, I think his exact words were, 'Does Kai know that?'"

"I don't know," I mumbled. "How do you just drop that on someone after so long?"

"Go at your own pace," Trevor started.

"No. That's a terrible idea," Ivy interrupted. "His own pace had him moving to Florida, getting married and divorced, hightailing it to California, and having a baby. All just to avoid the truth."

"First," I frowned, "how do you know all that? Second, I wasn't *just* avoiding Kai. Things with my mom were fucked up and I had to get away from here."

"Emory is a great information gatherer, and he shares what he learns." Ivy shrugged. "And I'll give you the running from parent shit; I understand that at a level I don't even want to delve into. But you have to admit you were also avoiding Kai."

I huffed but finally nodded. "So, how do I tell him?"

Ivy shook his head. "Don't know, man. But I think you need to make it a goal. Something like before the new year you'll be honest with him."

"That's a good idea," Trevor said.

Blowing out a long breath, I worked to control the panic. "That's just over a month away."

"Plenty of time. Straight up kiss him, rip the Band-Aid off. Or sit him down and tell him exactly how you feel." Ivy flipped off the main light switch. "Christmas can be all romantic and shit; make it one to remember."

Trevor snorted and rolled his eyes. "Maybe don't take romance advice from Scrooge over here."

"Your brother likes my big—"

"Lalalalala," Trevor chanted, sticking his fingers in his ears. "I can't hear you."

"My big romantic heart," Ivy finished loudly with a laugh. "Get your mind out of the gutter."

Trevor removed his fingers from his ears and eyed his best friend suspiciously.

"Em likes my big dick too," Ivy quipped and ducked Trevor's fist, almost falling over he laughed so hard.

I let myself focus on their antics for the time being.

Because if I let my head and heart start thinking about telling Kai the truth, I'd possibly hyperventilate.

CHAPTER 7

KAI

"Have you seriously never told him you're in love with him?" Emory asked as he, Blake, and I set the table.

"What? Who?" I attempted to deflect. Part of me wished I was outside with Colby, but we didn't have the baby monitor with us, so I'd opted to keep an ear on Elsie.

Emory rolled his eyes and cocked a hip. "Don't play dumb. Smart people who play dumb suck at it."

I sighed. "Don't know what good it would do. He's straight. We've been friends for twenty-five years. If he had some sort of feelings for me, I would have known." I put the last knife next to a plate. "He's my best friend and I don't *need* more than that. I'd rather have him in my life like this than lose him completely."

Blake rested his hands on the back of a dining room chair. "What makes you think you'd lose him? I mean, I don't think *every* pair of best friends ends up falling for each other, obviously—unless you're reading those best-friends-to-lovers romance novels Trevor says Emory reads —but it's easy to see you two have that spark. Isn't it a shame to never see if it could be something more?"

With my heart begging to agree, I shrugged. "Just don't want to make things weird. He was my rock when I was figuring out I was bi. Last thing I want to do is put him in an awkward position and be the cliché bi guy falling for his straight best friend."

Emory took hold of my hand. "First, those books are good. Everyone should read romance. Second, don't worry about stereotypes and clichés. Society spends way too much time trying to pigeon-hole people with specific labels and roles. Who you love doesn't have to meet any requirements. Forget all that." He stood in front of me and gripped my shoulders. "Be honest. Do you want to live your life with any other person by your side?"

Swallowing thickly, I shook my head.

"Look, if I couldn't see the way that man looks at you, I wouldn't be gunning for you to spill your feelings and possibly make things weird," Emory said, pushing his glasses up his nose. "But we can all see it. He has feelings for you. You owe it to him and yourself to at least be honest. Maybe you try things and decide you're better as friends. Maybe you give it a go and realize it's your dream come true. But you both need to have the chance to make that decision."

The door opened and voices floated in. Forcing myself to take a deep breath and push away the conversation—as well as the inkling of hope doing its damnedest to take root in the depths of my soul—I glanced toward Trevor, Ivy, and Colby walking into the dining room.

A spike of jealousy shot through me as Ivy wrapped an arm around Emory, pulling him close for a kiss. Trevor blushed as Blake leaned in and brushed their lips together.

God, I wanted that with Colby.

Instead, I smiled when he bumped his shoulder into me. "Elsie still asleep?"

"Yeah, we should be able to get through dinner."

Emory clapped his hands. "Okay, the food is ready. Let's eat."

The six of us enjoyed a delicious meal and nearly made ourselves sick laughing at the most ridiculous shit. Ivy and Trevor had the same easy friendship I had with Colby —the shared years between them were evident. Emory and his brother adored each other, and it made me wish I'd had siblings.

Then there were Ivy and Emory. I didn't know their whole story, but I had a theory. They definitely had the whole *he fell first, but he fell harder* vibe going on. Emory had likely been crushing on his older brother's best friend for years. Ivy had been dealing with shit from his past and just going along being friends with Trevor, and then *bam*, he started seeing Emory in a different light.

And what about Trevor and Blake? Trevor hadn't ever been into guys. Okay, maybe he hadn't realized it or let himself accept it. That was one of the issues with heterosexuality being the damn default in our society. Then he'd met Blake and *boom* he started questioning everything.

But that did *not* mean Colby felt anything other than friendship for me. I'd protect him and Elsie with my life. He could piss me off quicker than anyone else, but there was also no one I'd rather spend my time with. Sure, I had detailed fantasies about what I'd love to do with him if we ever found ourselves in a naked experimenting-type situation, but I did *not* need anything sexual with him to continue loving him more than my own damn life.

Do you really think Colby is just going to keep hanging around and playing house with you?

No.

I didn't.

But I also didn't want to tell him how I felt and have him stay out of a weird sense of guilt or obligation because I wanted him in ways that fell far outside of friendship.

I understood what Emory was saying. It wasn't fair to keep my feelings to myself and not let Colby have the chance to make his own choices.

The only problem was having no idea how he'd respond.

I knew he'd never get angry or be disgusted that I found him attractive. Colby had never been like that. But I worried he'd overthink things, get weird, and a wedge would grow between us. I couldn't deal with that.

As the six of us cleared the table, joking about how smart it was to use disposable plates and utensils, Elsie fussed from the other room just as a knock sounded at the door.

"I'll get her," I said.

The grateful warmth in Colby's eyes went straight to my gut, but I ignored it and headed to get the baby as Ivy went toward the door.

Twenty minutes later, Elsie was dry and fed. She made

cooing noises on my knee and giggled at Magic as she reached her tiny, chubby hands out to touch the dog.

Francis had stopped by with sugar cream pie and offered to trade it for a cup of coffee. Grateful our new friends weren't the type to turn away a lonely old man, I smiled as I took in the table. Steaming mugs of coffee, sugar cream pie, and a found-family vibe I hadn't even realized I needed.

My parents were great, but having this group of men in my life was proving to be more than I could have ever hoped for.

Francis was well into a story about his late partner. "We never married. In the beginning, it was because we weren't allowed to. Then, we just never got around to it." The old man got a far-off look in his eyes. "Back when I was just a kid, I never would have imagined I could *ever* marry a man." He smiled, lost in a memory. "Oh, but if I could have back then, I would have married my best friend, Sammy. Would have told him how much I loved him, grabbed him for a kiss, and married him before we shipped off to war."

The table grew quiet, Francis traveling through the past.

He shook his head. "Sammy was my everything. We never talked about it, but I felt it in my core that we both fancied men—and had a thing for each other. Not only could we not marry, we couldn't even be together as more than friends. Going to war, coming home, settling down, starting a family—those were the things expected of us." Francis's hand shook as he sipped his coffee. "I regret not telling him I loved him every single day." He sighed. "Don't get me wrong, I loved Jonathan and we shared a good life. But I lost the love of my life when Sammy and I went off to war. He never came home, and I came home broken and alone. For so many years, I simply existed. Then I met Jonathan and things were good." Francis closed his eyes. "But I miss Sammy every day and wish like hell I'd been honest with him."

I was grateful when the story finished, and I could pretend it hadn't affected me. It was easier to just go with the flow as we all chatted and finished our dessert for the next few moments before Francis slapped his hands against the tabletop and stood. "Well, it's time for me to head out. Thank you, gentlemen, so kindly for humoring an old man. Please don't feel bad for me, I had a happy life, and I'm still kicking." He glanced at Ivy and Emory, Trevor and Blake, and then turned a cocked brow toward Colby and me. "Just seeing such happy couples reminds me of what Sammy and I weren't allowed to have. Partly because of the time period, partly because I didn't dare tell him the truth."

His words were like a punch to my gut, and I handed Elsie to her dad so I could busy myself with gathering the last of the dishes. I didn't think any of the guys had put Francis up to telling us that story, but that almost made it worse. What was I supposed to do with the story—especially when Francis gave Colby and me such a pointed look? Grab Colby and tell him I didn't want to have regrets like Francis? Spend the rest of my life knowing I was going to turn out like the older man? He'd been happy; I could be happy.

Without Colby?

Fuck.

I headed to the bathroom for a quick breather.

I'd spent Black Friday helping Emory decorate his place. The vintage holiday decorations, the story about the mysteriously appearing mistletoe, and the seemingly living snow globe were fascinating—not to mention the other things he and Ivy had discovered in the house—and we'd enjoyed a day of building a friendship around the spirit of the holiday.

Ivy and Colby had grilled burgers and hot dogs despite the chill in the air, and Trevor and Blake had shown up after the decorating was done. Even though we'd spent Thanksgiving Day together, the six of us had enjoyed another meal and talked into the evening until we needed to get Elsie home and to bed. Colby had offered to take her home so I could stay, but the thought of the two of them going home without me didn't sit well.

So, we'd trekked across the little side road and worked together to get Elsie bathed, dressed, fed, and asleep. Then Colby and I had lounged on the couch, shoulders pressed together as we watched a movie on the laptop— something that had quickly become one of my favorite things we did.

Colby had jostled me awake a bit later. "Better head to bed. She'll want a bottle in a couple hours."

And she had. Elsie Mae screamed her head off a while later, and we fell into our nightly routine of diaper change and a bottle. I didn't *have* to get up with Colby. He told me nightly. I knew he could handle it. But I loved those moments of teamwork, the quiet blanketing the room as the cries finally subsided and the only noise was that of the baby chugging her bottle.

The best part, aside from watching my best friend love his daughter, was that Colby fell back asleep quickly. Which meant when he got super cuddly in his sleep, I could pretend, even for just a few minutes until sleep overtook me, that he knew he was pulling me close to him and holding me in his arms.

With his arm around my chest, his legs tangled with mine, and his face pressed into my neck, everything was right. We were CoJack, taking on the world together, raising our little girl, loving each other, and conquering each day.

Together.

And every morning, waking in Colby's arms was the best and worst.

The best because of how good he smelled. His warm strength. The promise that something amazing was coming our way.

The worst because we pretended it didn't happen. Separated quickly; a chill spreading across skin when our bodies no longer touched.

That morning, the day Emory and I would decorate my house, started the same, and I wanted to beg the universe for the chance to make things different. Even if just for that moment in time.

One time to roll in Colby's arms and press our mouths together.

To touch him the way my body longed for.

To whisper in his ear that I wanted to collect on the deal we'd had. Wanted to give it a shot and see what we could be.

Because I loved him.

Instead, I'd played the game of not realizing we were

wrapped together, bolted from bed muttering something about needing to pee, and showered. By the time I'd jerked myself off to visions of my best friend, and dressed for the day in a long-sleeved shirt and jeans, Colby had Elsie in the kitchen eating oat cereal and sweet potatoes.

I bent and kissed Elsie's head, skirting away when one little orange hand flailed my way. Picturing how easy it would be to kiss Colby, I messed his bed head. He laughed and elbowed me in the gut.

Things we'd done with each other almost daily for a quarter of a century.

Completely the same.

Yet so vastly different.

For one, Colby made faces at Elsie while he spooned her breakfast into her.

Second, my entire being longed for him. True, that wasn't much different than what I'd felt since I was sixteen. However, seeing Colby as a father, waking up with him, sharing space with him day in and day out was absolute pleasure and torture all rolled into one.

After breakfast, a bright-eyed and bushy-tailed Emory showed up at the door. Once Colby had helped us carry boxes up from the basement, he slapped me on the back. "I'm going to bundle Elsie up and take her over to Ivy's; he's going to change the oil on my truck. You two have fun."

Emory clapped his hands together and eyed the boxes labeled Christmas. "Let's get this party started."

"I don't think we have anything nearly as old, as cool, or as plentiful as the decorations your house had," I said as I lifted one lid. "Mom didn't keep a lot of things and the people who lived here before us didn't leave much from what my parents said."

"No worries, I just love to decorate. We can always go shopping for more if needed." Emory dug into a box.

"Main thing I want is a tree with lights. I've got this crazy idea of watching Elsie with the lights." I shrugged. "Probably stupid, but the thought of her being mesmerized by the pretty lights is just the perfect image in my mind."

"That makes sense and I'm sure it will happen," Emory said. "She's starting to be fascinated by her surroundings. She's in love with Magic. I bet her pretty little face will glow and her eyes will sparkle when she sees the lights."

That.

That was exactly what I pictured when I thought of Christmas with Colby and Elsie. I knew she wouldn't have a single clue as to what was going on this year, but I wanted to see the holiday glow through her eyes.

With Colby by my side.

Fuck.

I was setting myself up for the biggest fall.

Once we'd gone through the boxes, we had a decent number of decorations to start with. A nice little tree, silver icicles, teal blue lights, silver tinsel, along with silver, blue, and white snowflakes, and a silver snowflake topper. The tree skirt was silver, blue, and white. The tree would look nice with what we had available, but I couldn't figure out why there were only three round ball ornaments: two teal and silver and one white and silver.

"This is great," Emory said as he organized the decorations. "I think we need to get some white lights."

"And more ornaments," I said. "I'm going to have Mom come look at this stuff. Maybe seeing it will jog her memory as to where she might have put the rest of it."

Emory and I stopped for lunch and spent about an hour with Ivy, Colby, and Elsie before Mom showed up. Colby headed over to see his Dad and Allison, Ivy went back to work, and Emory hung out with Mom and me.

"I swear, Kai, I've never in my life seen those decorations," Mom said, hands on her hips as she stared at the silver, white, teal, and blue items.

"Mom," I huffed. "We got them from the basement. Maybe you bought them one year and just forgot."

She shook her head. "They're gorgeous, but I would have bought a lot more of the ornaments, not just three of them. The snowflakes and icicles will look great, but I'm one hundred percent positive those aren't our decorations."

I let it go because there was no use arguing with her, but by the time she left, I was beyond frustrated. "Where the heck does she think all that stuff came from?" I asked Emory as we drove to the store. "It didn't just *appear* in our basement."

Em smirked. "Ivy would tell you not to get me started on holiday magic…"

I rolled my eyes. "I know this whole town is supposedly full of it, and I know you're all about it, but it makes a lot more sense that my parents bought that stuff and forgot about it than trying to explain it away with Christmas magic."

Emory nodded, his big brown eyes blinking innocently behind the lenses.

"I'm serious, Em. Maybe my dad bought it and put it

down there. Or he got it at some yard sale and just forgot to tell Mom. There are like a hundred possibilities that are more likely than magic."

We headed into the discount store a couple towns over. Emory grabbed a cart and beelined toward the holiday décor, seemingly content to let the *magic* conversation go.

It wasn't that I *didn't* believe in Christmas magic, I was just practical enough to realize there were a lot of answers that made more sense.

"Ohhhh," Emory said. "Great sale on these lights." He placed three boxes of white lights into the cart.

After scanning the round ornaments, I finally sighed in defeat. "No teal or white like the ones we have. Maybe I'll just get different colors altogether."

"No, no, no," Emory said in a rush. "Look, there are teal, silver, blue, and white bows. Those will look great with the snowflakes and icicles."

I didn't disagree, so I grabbed the silky ribbon ornaments and we headed toward the checkout.

Two hours later, Emory and I were putting the finishing touches on the indoor decorations when Colby and Elsie got home.

Colby whistled. "This place looks amazing."

A small nativity adorned the fireplace, a wreath hung on the front door, a lighted wicker snowman lit up the front steps, a Christmas candle permeated the air with fresh pine, and a sprig of mistletoe hung from the doorway.

But the main attraction was the Christmas tree. It wasn't the traditional red and green, but the silver, teal, blue, and white spread a wintery glow across the living room. The tree sparkled, the tinsel doing a bang-up job of being festive.

Emory had convinced me to let him position the three lonely ornaments on the tree, and I had to admit they looked cute nestled into the branches.

"You know, Magic got his name because of all the things that happened in our house last season," Emory said to Colby in a suggestive tone.

"Aside from my mom forgetting about these decorations, nothing weird is happening here," I said, trying to preempt Emory getting back in magic mode.

Emory shook his head. "Christmas magic isn't about weird things happening. It's about what you feel in your heart." He glanced between Colby, Elsie, me, and the tree. "I'm pretty sure there's plenty of magic here if you just let it happen."

Thanks, Emory. Let's just make things awkward.

Colby cleared his throat. "Like those three ornaments?"

I wasn't sure if he was trying to change the subject, but I took the bait.

"We couldn't find any more, but Emory was determined they'd look okay by themselves," I explained.

Colby moved closer to the tree and Elsie squealed, her chubby hands flailing and her little legs churning a mile a minute.

Emory gasped and pulled out his phone. After snapping a picture, he moved to show us what he'd captured. "Call it magic or fate or history or whatever you want, but this picture proves the three of you have it. Look at that baby's eyes glowing in the lights." He bumped his shoulder against mine. "Just like you imagined." Pointing at the three ornaments, he hummed a little Christmas tune.

A few minutes later, as he headed for the door, Emory nodded his chin toward the tree. "It's almost like the ornaments are the three of you. If you believe in that type of thing."

CHAPTER 8

COLBY

COMING BACK TO PEPPERMINT HOLLOW HAD been the best decision of my entire life.

And the worst.

Building on the foundation my dad and I had established once he got his shit together all those years ago allowed for healing I didn't even realize I needed. Allison was an amazing person, so very good for Dad, and I appreciated the way she fit so seamlessly into her role in my life. Seeing my father become a grandpa—the way he effortlessly became Papaw Tom—did funny things to my heart. He'd messed up with me back when I was a kid— thanks in part to the horrendous person who was my mother—but he'd worked his ass off to fix things with me, and he was determined to be everything Elsie needed in a grandpa.

I wasn't *glad* I'd had a shit childhood, but getting a second chance with my dad, and watching him get a redo with my daughter was almost worth it.

And who knew I needed the whole found-family vibe

as badly as I did? When I left Peppermint Hollow, I was running from the shit my mom saddled me with. I had a tentative relationship with my dad. I had my best friend. I didn't need anything else. I planned to push everything bad away, find a girl to love as much as I loved Kai, and build an amazing life.

Well, while all of that went to shit, I'd evidently missed out on the fact I was lonely as hell. I had Kai, of course. Things were good with Dad. But my circle of friends was nothing but a dot. Coming home, meeting Emory, Ivy, Trevor, and Blake—finding myself building *true* friendships with people who shared my values and were so damn easy to spend time with—that had been one of the most unexpected positives of being back in town.

Reconnecting with Kai's parents had been a huge plus as well. For much of my childhood, Eric and Lacy Jackson had been the love and support I didn't have at home. I wasn't sure what they thought of Kai bringing Elsie and me into his home, but they adapted without even a moment's hesitation. They doted on Elsie as much as Dad and Allison did, and I could only laugh at how worried I'd been when I thought my baby wouldn't have family around.

Even the Peppermint Hollow folks had been good to me since I came back. Sure, there were the expected side-eyed looks and whispers, but most were kind and welcoming. We'd lucked out that someone who knew our families had suggested Keelie as a babysitter. The town was the usual small-town gossip-fest, but overall, they were good people—accepting Emory and Ivy, Blake and Trevor, providing the little rainbow stickers and flags—it gave me hope that Elsie would grow up in an open-minded, safe place.

And then there was Kai.

What could I even say? The man was above and beyond in every single way. No one, especially me, deserved a friend like Kai. But I'd somehow won the fucking best friend lottery. It was no wonder I'd gone and fallen in love with him.

But what was I supposed to do about it?

It wasn't fair to let him house us, co-parent my child, and give up his social life for me. Kai didn't date a lot, but he'd stopped dating completely ever since we'd moved in. I didn't like the thought of him dating, but I also felt guilty if I was cramping his style.

On the other hand, maybe Ivy and Trevor were right, and I needed to just be honest with Kai about how I felt. More than likely, he'd just do his best to let me down gently, and we'd go on with our lives. I'd need to find a place to live sooner rather than later. The thought of moving out sent a deep ache straight to my soul. Faking sleep and pulling him into my arms every night after we got Elsie back to bed; pretending not to realize how we woke wrapped together every morning. The end of those things—the end of just spending my days with him— would hurt. But I knew I'd never completely lose my best friend.

As long as I didn't go and make things weird between us.

My mind teetered back and forth between taking Ivy and Trevor's advice and being honest with Kai, or just keeping my feelings to myself like I'd done for so many years. The guys had suggested doing it before Christmas. I had offered up that stupid deal of *if we're still single at thirty* to Kai way back when. Maybe I'd let things ride for now. If an opportunity presented itself—or if Kai let on he felt anything more than friendship—I'd jump on it. If not, at least I'd have Kai in my life.

If the universe had some big plan for us, I was ready and willing.

I ran a hand over my face. Peppermint Hollow was getting to me. I'd never been one to credit fate or hand things over to the universe. It was all Emory's talk of holiday magic and those three ornaments being Kai, Elsie, and me. Don't get me wrong, I thought they were cute as hell, and I loved thinking of our little trio as a family up there on the tree, but still, the holiday magic stuff was doing weird shit to my head.

After changing Elsie's diaper late one morning about a week after Kai and Emory decorated, I walked with her into the living room and paused. Something was different.

Stockings.

"I like the stockings," I called to Kai.

"I figured you did since you got them," he said with a smirk as he joined us near the fireplace.

"What? I didn't get them. I thought you did."

Three stockings hung from the mantle. They matched the three ornaments on the tree perfectly and each silken stocking had a name.

Kai, Elsie, Colby.

"Seriously? You didn't get them?" Kai asked.

I shook my head.

"I bet it was Em. He hasn't completely given up on getting us to believe in the Christmas magic." Kai shook his head. "I'll get him to confess."

An hour later, Emory and Ivy were at the house and the younger man was swearing on his life he didn't put up the stockings.

Ivy shrugged. "I can't say for sure, but I definitely haven't seen him with stockings or sneaking over here to decorate your fireplace."

"Well, *someone* put them there," I said with a huff.

Ivy slapped me on the back. "Sometimes, it's easier to just let the magic do its work."

I sighed. "At least they match."

Emory beamed.

Later that day, we headed over to Blake's place to eat lunch with him and Trevor, but cut the visit short because Elsie was fussy.

She went down easily for a nap after her bottle, but the rest of the day was an absolute shit-show. Kai and I took turns holding her; she screamed if we put her down. She didn't want food, she kept pulling off her bottle, and she fussed while rubbing her head against our chests.

We tried everything to help soothe her. Two grown men were in an absolute tizzy because our normally easy-going baby was out of sorts, but damn it, we were determined to get her calmed down.

Finally, after reading through lists of possible problems in our book and checking in with our parents, we decided maybe she was teething. Her gums weren't red and we didn't feel anything trying to pop through, but it was a viable option.

So, we put her in her chair and gave her a little mesh pocket with a frozen mango. That kept her somewhat happy for about twenty minutes, and we mistakenly thought we were out of the woods.

No such luck.

The screaming started again as Kai cleaned up the mango mess. "What about the shower? She likes the sound usually, and maybe the warm water will feel good?"

At that point, I knew we'd both agree to absolutely anything just to try to make her stop crying. The heartbreaking part was this wasn't the fussiness we saw here and there from time to time. Elsie was a hot mess, and I was helpless to do anything. She couldn't tell us what was wrong and I'd never felt so worthless in my life.

"Can you get in with her first?" I asked. "I want to get on the app and see if we can get an appointment with her doctor first thing in the morning. The blog said it's always better to be safe than sorry."

Kai nodded and took Elsie from me.

By the time I confirmed a late morning appointment for the next day—thank god for a pediatrician's office that had multiple doctors and nurse practitioners—Kai had Elsie in the shower.

Fuck.

We'd showered with her before. Sometimes it was quicker and easier to just let the spray rain down than do a whole bath. But we'd always done it by ourselves, not as a group thing.

Kai's body on display through the glass doors was a work of art.

If I hadn't been so concerned about my baby, I would have spent forever watching him. As it was, at that moment, Elsie started to fuss and flail again.

"Fuck," Kai said. "She slippery. Can you take her? I'll dry off and grab her so you can shower. I have a feeling it's going to be a long night."

Dear god, we had no idea.

Averting my eyes from Kai's very gorgeous, very masculine body I wanted to run my hands all over, I took Elsie in a towel and held her close. Giving Kai some privacy—mostly so I wouldn't pop wood right there in the bathroom while I watched him like some perv—I walked Elsie around and hummed one of her bedtime songs.

Did babies just have bad days? Maybe it was just one of those. A good night's sleep would help.

Right?

Kai padded toward me, his caramel hair damp, the thatch on his chest still wet. "I'll rock her. Shower. This is definitely a two-person tag-team match tonight."

Never had a shower been so fast and filled with the weirdest combination of thoughts—worry for my baby, a ramped-up desire for my best friend, and confusion over what the hell I should do with these feelings.

All I knew was guilt rained down on me. Guilt over being a shit dad who couldn't help his baby. Guilt over wanting Kai so badly, even considering dropping that bomb, when I knew damn well I had no business getting into another relationship. Especially not one with my lifelong best friend.

Fuck.

I just needed Elsie to sleep off whatever the issue was and get our little routine back in order. When things were normal, I could figure shit out better.

After a quick shower, I found Kai giving Elsie her bedtime bottle a little early. The bedroom was dark, the sound machine on, and Elsie was snug in her pjs.

"Figured she didn't nap worth a darn today so maybe starting bedtime early would help," Kai spoke softly.

"Is she taking the bottle?" I kept to the shadows of the bedroom and pulled on boxer briefs, sweats, and a t-shirt.

"She's trying. She sucks on it and then pulls off. It's like she's hungry, but something hurts?"

After sending a text to Lacy, I thumbed through the parenting book.

"Fever?" I asked. "God, I didn't even think about a fever."

Kai bent and put his cheek against her head. How many times had Lacy checked Kai or me for a fever that way? "She doesn't feel warm. Maybe get the thingy."

Knowing exactly what he meant, I hurried to the medicine box and pulled out the thermometer. Elsie was *not* a fan of the thermometer going in her ear, but it worked quickly. "No fever."

"Your mom wants to know if she's pulling at her ears?" I asked.

Kai bit his lip. "Yeah. It started with rubbing her face on us, but now she keeps messing with that one."

"Shit." I sent back the answer and waited for the reply. "Your mom says, 'Sounds like an ear infection. Or at least the beginning of one. Give her baby Tylenol for the pain. Fever will likely start later. Doctor will probably give antibiotics tomorrow.' Shit," I muttered. "I didn't even think about Tylenol."

"It's okay, we've never had to give it to her. Let's get her some and see if that helps. Maybe we can get in front of the fever." Kai placed the bottle aside. "We'll see if she wants this once the pain is better."

I rummaged through the medicine box and pulled out the baby Tylenol. Luckily, the directions were crystal clear, and Elsie seemed to like the taste because she slurped it right down.

"I know fevers are bad, but I feel like I've also read it's better to let a fever play out," I said as I took my baby and cuddled her close. "I don't want her to be sick, but if a fever helps get rid of stuff..."

"We can ask the doctor tomorrow," Kai said. "Main thing is we relieve her pain and get her to sleep for now." He patted my cheek with a wink and a tired smile. "He says with absolutely no fucking clue what he's talking about."

I chuckled. "You and me both. I didn't realize how lucky we've been that she's not been sick until now."

"And how does an ear infection just *bam* show up?"

"Right?" I settled into the rocker.

Kai brought over a blanket and placed it over me, tucking it around my shoulders, and covering Elsie's little butt as she curled against me. "Guess it's one of those things that parents deal with, but *damn*, this is nerve-wracking."

"I'm sorry you have to deal with this," I said.

"Shut up," Kai interrupted. "We help each other. It's what we've done for years. Remember when you finished my science project for me because I was puking all over the place in sixth grade?"

I chuckled at the memory. "And then I got whatever you had and ended up missing school, but you presented my project *and* yours."

"We both got A's if I remember correctly."

I nodded, rocking Elsie gently, my hand patting her back. "We did." The day was catching up with me and a wave of emotion blanketed me. "Thank you. For then, and for now."

"It's what we do." He touched my shoulder. "Are you going to put her down or sleep with her there?"

Hesitating, I glanced at her bed. "Sick babies are a total mind-fuck. I want her comfortable and near me, but sleeping in the chair isn't the safest option."

Kai moved Elsie's little bed closer to my side of the bed. "She's in warm pajamas and has her little sleep sack thing on. The house is set at seventy-three."

I liked how he just gave me information and didn't try to sway me one way or another. Nodding, I slowed the rocker and stood slowly. The medicine seemed to be working because my exhausted little girl was conked out. Gently placing her on her back in her bed, I held my breath and hoped she'd stay asleep. When she didn't stir, I stood with a sigh of relief.

Kai shut off the tiny lamp on his side of the bed. "I know it's not super late, but I'm so damn tired. And if it's an ear infection, that medicine is only good for like four hours I think."

Running a hand over my face, I groaned. "Need to sleep. Gonna get another bottle set up first. She didn't take that bedtime one, so she'll either wake in pain or hungry." I winced. "Or both."

"Shit," Kai grumbled. "This stuff isn't for the weak. I'll get another dose of medicine ready, and all the diaper stuff laid out."

We'd made late-night diapers and bottles a pretty easy routine by being prepared, and it helped to ease some of the anxiety of a sick baby by sticking to the routine as much as possible.

We set off in the dark, quiet house. I checked the thermostat while Kai locked the doors. Peppermint Hollow wasn't a town with much crime, but it was still a habit we'd gotten into.

By the time we'd both done our part of the preparations, used the bathroom, and brushed our teeth, I was about to drop. Checking on Elsie, sending up a prayer that she slept for as long as possible, I climbed into bed.

My usual act of faking sleep and pretending I didn't realize I was cuddling Kai went into action much quicker. With a slight snore, I rolled toward him, and waited for his breathing to even out. He wasn't completely asleep, but we always joked about how quickly I drifted off, so I knew he'd think I was out.

God, I needed him in my arms. Needed his warmth, the press of his body against mine. I made my move and forced myself not to press kisses against his neck.

As usual, he tensed for a brief moment. The first time I dared to hold him while we slept, we were in college and drunk off our asses. Kai always froze and held his breath for just a second, before relaxing into the embrace. Never wanting to put him in an uncomfortable position, I was sure to keep the hold loose so he could easily roll away.

He never did.

With Elsie sound asleep and my arms full of my best friend, I breathed him in deeply. The best and worst part of this faking sleep so I could hold him in our sleep game I'd been playing for so many years was two-part. One, he thought I was asleep and didn't know what I was doing. Two, I had to decipher some of the things Kai did when he thought I was asleep.

The way he sometimes took my hand and pressed his

lips to my knuckles. The way he'd cuddle in, pressing his ass against me. The deep sigh as his body melted.

We'd always been comfortable with each other and free with touches. Part of me figured Kai just played along or enjoyed the cuddles. I knew Kai was a cuddler—one of his biggest complaints about people he hooked up with or dated was when they didn't like to cuddle. Or the few times he wasn't interested, but they turned into an octopus.

A tiny part of my mind kept reminding me that Kai just liked the closeness of another body, and who better than a lifelong friend?

But another minuscule voice whispered ever so softly. *Maybe Kai likes you. Maybe he wants to touch you as much as you want to touch him. Maybe he feels that same hot burn in his chest, the butterflies in his gut, when he thinks about you.*

It was ridiculous.

I knew it was.

Mostly.

But warm, sleepy bodies wrapped together had my brain going haywire.

And don't even get me started on my dick.

No. It was not the time for thoughts like that.

Elsie was sick. We needed rest.

I'd give more thought to telling my best friend I was in love with him later.

Kai sighed and snuggled closer, and sleep overtook me.

CHAPTER 9

KAI

SOMETHING WOKE ME.

I froze, listening.

It was after midnight and the room was quiet except for soft waves crashing on the sound machine.

There it was again.

What was that?

I sat up just as Elsie whimpered.

Colby bolted upright. "What's wrong?"

I scrambled from bed, switching on the small lamp, and Colby swung his feet to the floor next to Elsie's bed.

"Fuck, what's wrong with her?" Colby asked, his words so panicked and pained my chest ached for him.

Elsie's tiny body shook, shivers traveling through her as she whimpered.

"We're going to the ER." I grabbed my jeans and shoved my legs into them.

"Is she having a seizure?" Colby asked, picking Elsie up and holding her close. "Why isn't she crying?"

Yanking a hoodie over my head, I reached for a wad of

socks and pulled them on. Slipping into slides, I pocketed my phone. "I don't know, Cole, but I don't think babies shake like that. Is she hot?"

Colby's words cracked. "Yeah, she's burning up."

"Get dressed. Make sure you have your insurance card." I took Elsie. "I'm going to take her temperature so we can tell the doctor and then give her Tylenol."

Colby stood helplessly in the middle of the room.

I pulled him close to me, our foreheads pressing together. "Cole, get dressed. We need to go."

Terrified.

I was terrified.

I hadn't been around babies a lot, but watching Elsie shake and hearing her sad little whimpery noises broke my heart and sent ice racing through my veins.

Colby was worse off than me. She was my daughter in every sense of the word and I'd fight anyone who argued. But she was Colby's flesh and blood. He'd watched her be born; a living, breathing piece of his heart, and she was sick.

Elsie had stopped the shivery shakes by the time I got the thermometer and the baby Tylenol. She was screaming at the top of her lungs by the time I took her temperature —which was a frightening 103.4 degrees. Luckily, she took the medicine easily before I stripped her from the sleep sack and wrapped her in a blanket.

Colby was dressed and ready.

"Here." I handed Elsie to him. "Do you have your wallet?"

Colby popped the pacifier into Elsie's mouth. "Yeah."

We reached the kitchen where I grabbed the makings for the bottle, stuffed them in the diaper bag, and shoved my wallet in my pocket. Jangling my keys, I said, "I'll drive."

"Shit, the car seat," Colby mumbled.

Fuck.

I hurried to where we left the seat sitting on the living room floor earlier and rushed back with it.

Elsie screamed her head off as we got her strapped in. Colby's soothing words were laced with fear and heartache. "God, I hate making her sit in this thing."

"She'll be safe and warm." I understood his reluctance, but the seat seemed the safest bet. "Let's go. You sit in the back with her so she can see you," I said.

As we headed toward my car, Blake sprinted over. "What's wrong?"

Startled, but too focused on Elsie, I answered quickly, "She's sick. We're going to the ER."

"Let me drive. Neither of you will be focused on the road." Blake took my keys before I could argue, and we all piled into the car.

"Thank you," Colby muttered as Blake backed out of the drive.

I'd climbed in the back with Colby, the baby carrier locked into the base between us. "It's nearly one in the morning, why were you outside?"

Blake caught my eye in the rearview mirror. "Coming home from Trevor's," he said with a grin. "When did she get sick?"

"Earlier today, she was fussy. Wouldn't eat, messing with her ears. We have an appointment with the pediatrician, but she woke up shaking," Colby explained, his left hand on Elsie's chest, one finger keeping the pacifier in her mouth.

I placed my hand over his, the fear evident in his tremor. "She has a fever of 103.4; I don't know if the shaking was from being cold or…"

"It was scary as fuck," Colby interjected. "Looked like a seizure. And she was just whimpering, not crying, like if she had teeth, they would have been chattering."

Blake kept us talking on the drive to the ER.

Elsie was back to sleep thanks to the Tylenol, and her fever was definitely at least a little lower.

"Shit man," Colby said as we neared the hospital. "How are you going to get home? Let me call my dad—"

"No worries, I'll get an Uber." Blake pulled into the ER drop-off zone. "I'll fill the guys in; keep us posted. Call if you need anything."

"Go on," I told Colby. "I'll park and be right in."

He released the car seat and hurried toward the sliding doors.

Blake got out and moved to the passenger side while I got in on the driver's side. As he entered his info on the ride-share app, I circled the lot looking for a place to park.

He walked with me toward the ER entrance.

"Thanks so much, man." I pulled him into a hug. "Neither of us were in the right frame of mind to drive."

He slapped me on the back. "No worries. Seriously, call if you need anything."

I left him in the little vestibule and hurried inside.

Colby was next in line. Elsie was screaming. He looked like he was about to cry.

I took the carrier and got Elsie quiet—thank god for pacifiers.

Maybe it was because of the way Colby looked. Maybe it was because it was a baby. Or maybe we just lucked out, but the lady at the check-in counter worked quickly and had someone come to take us right away.

"Parent or guardian only," the older nurse said as she met us with an electronic tablet.

My heart sank.

"I'm the father. This is my husband," Colby said, his words strong and determined.

And then my heart stopped.

Colby's free hand took mine. I wondered if the nurse recognized the extreme stubbornness on his face as he jutted his chin as if waiting for her to say I couldn't come.

"Come on, then," she said, leading us to a tiny cubicle-type space with three walls and a curtain across from what seemed to be a station or hub for nurses and doctors.

Colby sat on the bed with the carrier by his side and I took the chair in the corner, shoving the diaper bag underneath.

Therese took all the details we could give her and asked about a million questions. She was quick and efficient, perhaps not overly polite or comforting, but she got the job done.

"You can keep her in the carrier or hold her until the doctor comes in." She swiped a thermometer over Elsie's forehead. "They may want a rectal temperature reading later, but this will work for now. Her temp is down to 100, so the Tylenol is keeping her comfortable." Therese typed a few more things into her tablet and stood to leave.

After the curtain had been whipped closed, the rings noisily scraping across the rod, Colby leaned his arm over the carrier handle and rested his head on his elbow. "Fucking hell, Else," he whispered hoarsely. "Shit," he muttered, sitting back up. "We should have asked if she can take the bottle if she wakes up."

I stood. "I'm going to take a piss, I'll stop by and ask on my way back."

Colby just nodded, his eyes flat with fear and exhaustion. "Thanks."

Unsure if it was the right move—Colby claiming me as his husband earlier had done a number on my head—I moved to stand in front of him and pulled him into a hug. I'd hugged the man a million times over the years, but this time was different. This time we were scared silly about Elsie. We were exhausted. And we'd had months of cuddling together while we slept, growing the bond that had held us together for so many years, watching each other be a father to the most gorgeous baby in the world. And maybe it was wishful thinking on my part, but I swore Colby held me tighter. He was just terrified and tired, that was all it was.

"Thank you for being here," he mumbled into my shoulder.

I held him a bit longer before slipping from the small space and glancing around for the restrooms. As I made my way to where the sign indicated, I noticed a coffee machine. Based on the fact I could smell the burned, stale coffee wafting through the air, I didn't think it held much promise, but if we ended up being in the ER for long, it was maybe our only hope.

A thought hit me. Shit. What if we got admitted? Was Elsie sick enough to need to stay in the hospital?

The bathroom was a small one-person set-up, but luckily, no one was using it. Flushing the toilet and washing my hands, I took a long, deep breath. We'd cross that bridge if we got to that point.

As I headed back toward our little room, I couldn't help but think about Colby calling me his husband. I knew he'd only done it because they weren't going to let me in, but his words had gone straight to my heart.

And to my dick.

Which was fucked up since we had a sick baby at the ER, but the thoughts of what it would be like to be Colby's husband ran rampant through my mind. To cuddle with him in bed because we both knew exactly what was happening. To touch him, hold him, kiss him. God, I wanted to kiss him so damn bad.

I stopped for a moment to look at a little sign about antibiotic-resistant infections—damn, medical stuff was scary—when I heard the nurses at the station talking.

"I don't know, the little one that just came in isn't looking good."

"Yeah, if I had to guess, she may not make it." That three-pack-a-day voice belonged to Therese, no doubt.

What the fuck? Was Elsie sicker than we thought? How did they know she wasn't going to make it?

I rounded the wall and stepped to the counter. "Excuse me," I said, my voice cracking. "I shouldn't have been eavesdropping, but you also shouldn't be talking about patients. We haven't even seen a doctor yet, but you're talking about our baby not making it?"

Confused faces stared at me.

And then one of the nurses reacted. Her mouth formed an O. "Nooo. I'm so sorry. Oh my god, no. We weren't talking about patients." She bustled to a little shelf and pointed to a tray of plants. "The overnight shift has a green thumb, and we get plants brought in from other floors in hopes of saving them." She held up a tiny succulent. "We just got this one from a nurse on the day shift. We're good, but we're not miracle workers; not sure this little one is going to survive."

My brain worked to resolve the initial fear and the current embarrassment, and I stumbled over my words. "Oh, um, sorry about that. New dad here and I'm not functioning all that well."

Therese, not being *as* bad as I'd originally thought, smiled. "It's okay. You're right, we need to watch the words we use so misunderstandings don't happen." She nodded toward our little room. "The doctor is heading in now."

Giving a feeble little wave, I ignored my burning cheeks and rushed to follow the doctor into Elsie's room.

"Hi there," the older man said. "I'm Dr. Dunkirk. You're in luck, I used to have my own pediatric practice before I retired. A man can only play so much golf, so I take shifts here a few times a month. All the docs are good," he smiled warmly, "but I'm a bit biased to say I'm the best, at least with sick babies." He checked the tablet he held. "Mr. Burke?" He glanced back and forth between Colby and me.

"I'm Colby Burke." Colby stood and offered his hand. "This is my husband, Kai."

I shook the man's hand dumbly, my brain synapses misfiring at the repeated claim of me being Colby's husband.

"Okay, gentlemen, tell me what's going on with Elsie?" He peeked at her sleeping soundly. "I'm guessing we've got some baby Tylenol on board?"

"Yeah, her temperature was 103.4 when she woke up. I gave her the Tylenol before we left to come here."

"We have a doctor's appointment with her pediatrician tomorrow," Colby explained, "but she woke up shaking, kinda looked like a seizure, scared us to death."

"She's not going to be happy with me here in a minute, I'll need to do a quick exam and check her out." Dr. Dunkirk typed on his tablet. "The shaking very likely was just from the fever. 103 is pretty high; you know what it's like to get the shivers when you've got a fever." He tapped something else on the screen. "There are events known as febrile seizures. Those are often brought on by infection or fever. They're scary, as most seizures are, but harmless for the most part." He turned the tablet toward us. "Did the event look like this?"

We watched a short video of a child having what was labeled a febrile seizure on the screen. From the corner of my eye, I caught Colby shaking his head along with me. "No, nothing like that. Just shaking and making a little whimpering noise."

"Like if she had teeth, they would have been chattering," I added Colby's description from earlier.

"I'm going to go with just shakes from the fever. If you notice the seizure activity like you saw on the video in the future, definitely get in with your pediatrician. I'll send you home with some literature on what to do during febrile seizures. I'm leaning toward saying it wasn't seizure activity, but it's something to keep in the back of your minds if it were to continue."

"And if it *is*, it's not harmful?" I asked.

"Not harmful, but something the pediatrician will want to monitor. Many kids who have febrile seizures grow out of them." He put his tablet down. "Okay, I'm going to make her unhappy. Hate to do it, but I need to check her out."

Unhappy was an understatement; Elsie screamed bloody murder. Why wouldn't she? The doctor had Colby strip her down to her very wet diaper. He checked her tummy, listened to her breathing and her heart, and examined her eyes and nose. When he got to her ears, he clucked, "There's the culprit."

"Ear infection?" Colby asked.

"Bingo-bango. This right ear is pretty nasty. The left is getting there."

"The parenting book and his mom suggested it was probably that based on how she was acting. Not eating, pulling at the ear."

"Are ear infections common?" I asked.

"One of the most common illnesses in infants and children, for sure; they can come on in an instant it seems. I've had many a patient examined in the office with no ear infection and by the time they got the little one home, the pain and fever had started." He did one final check. "We'll get her started on antibiotics. Keep your appointment for tomorrow. If infections start to be recurrent for her, your pediatrician will likely refer you to an ENT for tubes, but that's a ways down the road and requires more than just a few infections." He brushed his hand over Elsie's head. "Sorry, little one, I'm all done."

Colby changed her diaper quickly. "Can she have the bottle?" He looked at me.

Shit. I'd forgotten to ask.

Dr. Dunkirk nodded. "She's probably hungry. Sucking

on the bottle hurts the ears, but the Tylenol is helping for now, so she can try."

As he finished typing and asked us which pharmacy we wanted to use, I mixed up the bottle. Colby got Elsie dressed and she was chugging the bottle within moments as I re-packed the diaper bag.

"Gentlemen, you've all had a rough night. Get the antibiotics started and she'll be good as new." He finished typing and tucked the tablet under his arm. "My son and his partner were new dads just like you not so long ago. Even with a pediatrician as a father, they were overwhelmed in the beginning with how scary a baby can be."

Something flamed to life deep in my chest.

And then shattered.

Dr. Dunkirk's son had an actual husband.

A real family.

I had nothing but make-believe.

No. I pushed the thought aside. Colby wasn't my husband, and Elsie wasn't my flesh and blood, but none of that made a difference in how *real* we were. He was my best friend. My soul mate. We had twenty-five years of friendship behind us.

The rambling thoughts of an exhausted mind were worthless.

Dr. Dunkirk wished us a happy holiday season, assured us the prescription had been sent, and went on his way.

Helping to get Elsie back in her carrier, I focused only on getting her home and feeling better. The rest of it would have to wait until I was clear-headed.

Maybe after Christmas.

It was nearing four o'clock in the morning when we

finally got home with the prescription. Risking waking her for the day, but begging the universe to let the darkness and illness be enough to get Elsie back to sleep easily, we changed her diaper, gave her Tylenol, and got the first dose of antibiotics into her. As I rocked her and topped her off with the last little bit of the bottle, Elsie's eyes drifted shut.

"I texted Dad and Allison. They're going to come over around seven. Figure she'll be up by then. They said they'll watch her for a while so we can sleep." Colby's words were laced with exhaustion.

"Perfect. I know we have work stuff, but I need at least a few hours before I can function without being a zombie."

"Same." He watched me put her down in her bed. "You're getting good at that. Used to be scared to lay her down."

"Practice." I yawned. "I'm going to collapse if I don't go to bed. You want a water?" I was pretty sure neither of us had anything to drink since the day before.

"Please."

I headed to the kitchen and returned to find Colby climbing into bed. Tossing his water on the bed, I made a quick trip to the bathroom, downed my water, and joined him.

"Today was shit," I muttered.

"It was. Thanks for being there with me." Colby rolled toward me and pulled me close. Kissing the top of my head, he said, "I'm lucky to have a friend like you."

Oh god.

What we had was so good, so right.

So special.

But it could be so much more.

Or my horny ass could destroy twenty-five years of friendship if I pushed for something my best friend didn't want.

"Nowhere else I would have rather been," I said.

We both snorted.

"Okay, home in bed with a sleeping baby would have been better than the ER, but you know what I mean."

That time, we fell asleep together, Colby's warm arms strong and protective around me.

I knew without a doubt why dating had never worked out for me. Didn't matter; guy, girl, non-binary, no one held a candle to Colby Burke in my heart.

CoJack forever drifted through my dreams.

CHAPTER 10

COLBY

In a haze, I got up with Elsie at half-past six; we'd only been asleep a couple hours. Kai got up with me despite me telling him to stay in bed.

By the time I had Elsie's diaper changed and a bottle ready, Dad and Allison had arrived like the cavalry. They were bright-eyed and bushy-tailed, ready to be grandparents for as long as Kai and I needed to sleep.

"I wasn't worth shit when you were sick," Dad said, a sad frown on his face. "Neither was your mom for that matter. But I'm here now. Go on, get some rest."

Heading upstairs after thanking them profusely and kissing Elsie on the head, I found a freshly showered Kai changing the sheets.

"Don't know why, but I wanted clean ones," he said. "Shower. You'll feel better. Then we get a couple more hours at least."

He was right, I did feel better after a shower, and the sheets were fresh and clean as I slipped into bed beside him. Kai's soft snores stopped when I threw an arm over him and pressed a kiss to the back of his head.

My heart ached with how badly I needed him to know what I felt. I knew he knew I loved him—just like I knew he loved me—our friendship was too strong for either of us to doubt that.

But I wasn't sure how much longer I could go on pretending.

Pretending that I didn't want to touch him and kiss him.

That I didn't want to call him my husband for real and not just to bypass shitty hospital rules.

Didn't want to make this little life we'd built together real, not just a convenience that would have to end at some point.

Instead, I savored the warmth of his body in my arms and drifted off to sleep with *CoJack forever* drifting through my dreams.

❧

"I know I'm about fifteen years too late for the sex talk," Dad started as we stood in the living room later in the afternoon.

Kai had gone with me to take Elsie to the pediatrician earlier in the day. The good news was her ears were already looking better. The better news was she was happy as a clam and back to being her cheery self.

Dad and Allison had lunch ready for us when we got home from the doctor, and we'd spent the whole meal oohing and ahhing over everything Elsie did. It was absolutely amazing how much better she was doing in less than twenty-four hours. Thank god for access to modern medicine.

After lunch, Allison and Kai headed to the grocery store to get ingredients for Christmas cookies, while Dad and I entertained Elsie.

My eyes grew wide at Dad's words, and I wondered immediately why I'd ever thought other kids were lucky to have their parents to turn to as kids; this felt like it was going to get awkward. "Dad, it's all good." I nodded to the baby he held. "Pretty sure I've got the logistics down."

Dad chuckled and hesitated before clearing his throat. "As much as I'd like to laugh it off and take the easy road, I spent too many years being a shitty father because I hid from my life and everything in it."

My gut clenched. "Dad, we've talked about this, we're good." We truly were at a good place, and I didn't want to rehash things.

"Colby, just let me get this out, okay?"

I gestured for him to continue.

"You're like me in a lot of ways," Dad started, his eyes briefly landing on me before moving to look at Elsie's sweet little head propped in the crook of his elbow.

Where the hell was he going with this?

"Difference is, I shut myself off from the problems by detaching and being a shit husband, shit parent, shit person all around."

"Dad, Mom was—"

He held up his free hand. "Your mom was a good person who got sucked in by the drugs and she made terrible choices. She was a huge part of my problems, but I had other options. Instead of being a father to you, I shut down and barely made it through my days." We'd discussed this all before, but it seemed like he needed to talk, so I let him go. "As long as I didn't let *anything* in, I didn't have to deal with my addict wife, the son I didn't even know, the jobs I couldn't keep, or the friends I'd lost." Dad took a deep breath. "You? You moved to Florida and California. In your determination to escape your mom, you ended up with some version of her. Twice."

I winced. "Damn, tell me how you really feel," I muttered.

"I'm not saying all of this to make you feel bad, I've got an actual point."

"Wanna get to it?" I asked with a huff.

"You ran from your mom, a shitty childhood, a detached father." Dad's eyes raised to meet mine. "And the feelings you have for your best friend."

I immediately scoffed, ready to tell him he was wrong, ready to deny it.

But Dad held up a hand. "You can tell me I'm full of shit, but hear me out."

Drawing in a deep breath, I nodded.

"I saw it. Way back when you and Kai were teens, I saw it." He ran his free hand through his hair. "Things with your mom were at their worst, I was as far away in my head as possible, but I still saw what the two of you had. What you'd always had, but it was more. If I'd been anything close to a good father back then, I would have told you it was okay. Would have educated myself about same-sex partnerships, made sure you were equipped to be safe, and taken comfort in my son finding his person to love." Dad shook his head. "Instead, I withdrew further into my hell as your mom got worse every single day. And before too long, you and Kai were off to college. Then you were gone—run off to Florida, to California." His eyes bored into mine. "Yes, you were running from your mom. From me. But can you honestly say you weren't running from Kai too?"

My mouth opened, ready to deny. Instead, words poured out of me I didn't realize I'd been dying to tell my dad. "I've loved him since we were five. I fell *in love* with him when I was eighteen, maybe even before. I thought leaving was the right thing. I was the product of a broken home with an addict mother and an absent father—"

Dad winced, but if we were putting it all out there, I had things to say.

"I didn't need to add in the drama of discovering I was bisexual and in love with my best friend. So yeah, I ran. And things turned to shit." I shrugged and looked at Elsie sleeping in my dad's arms. "Mostly. Some things worked out all right."

"And now?" Dad asked.

"Now? Nothing has changed. I'm not the guy who gets the happy ending, Dad."

"That's bullshit and you know it." He shifted Elsie in his arms, moving her to snuggle against his chest.

"If I was meant for happy endings, Mom would have picked me over drugs. *You* would have decided to be a father long before she was finally out of your life." Yeah, low blow, but it was the truth. "I wouldn't have ended up with younger versions of my addict mom." I paced the living room; I hadn't been prepared for a soul-wrenching heart-to-heart with my dad on only a few hours of sleep.

"You deserve happiness, Colby."

"I have what I deserve. I have the most gorgeous baby,

a job I love, and a best friend who lets me crash at his place until I get my bearings."

"You could have so much more, you *have* so much more if you'd just open your eyes and take a risk." He put himself between me and my pacing.

"Where is all this coming from?" Folding my arms across my chest, I fought the urge to walk out of the house and not come back until the tension was gone.

"You spent the first chunk of your life thinking you weren't wanted and didn't deserve happiness. Because of that, I'd argue you deserve it more than anyone." Dad rubbed Elsie's back. "I convinced myself way back then that my shitty life was punishment for the way I was with your mom and you, but I know better now."

I narrowed my eyes and waited.

"I know I was a piece of shit. I know you didn't *have* to work things out with me. I know I'm the luckiest man alive to have found Allison. And I know that life can be so much better if we just choose to believe—"

"Believe what, Dad? Believe that my best friend is pining away for me? Believe that I can just tell him I've been in love with him since we were teens? And he'll, what? Put everything on hold just for me? Stand by while I work through what it means that I'm in love with him? And what if we're only meant to be friends and my declaration ruins everything? I can't lose the only person who's been by my side every single day for twenty-five years." I took a long, shuddering breath. "I just can't."

"I can't promise Kai feels the same. I can't promise things will be easy," Dad said. "But I've seen the two of you together all these years—even when I wasn't involved…yeah, I know, I was *never* involved…I see the way he looks at you, the way he loves you right back." He put a hand on my shoulder. "Sometimes, I think we're all looking too hard, trying too hard, and missing what's right in front of our faces. He's right there; you have to grab on to what makes you happy—choose to believe you deserve it, because you *do*—and never let go."

Allison and Kai walked in the door, laughing over something they'd seen at the store. Dad gave me a wink and handed Elsie over. I followed him into the kitchen, his words a heavy weight on my heart.

Dad kissed Allison. "Come on, we need to head home."

She beamed up at him, true love in her eyes even after all these years, and something punched me in the gut. Dad had gotten a second chance at life. At love. He'd taken it, even when he'd not been looking for it or expecting it. Even when he'd thought he hadn't deserved it, love had still found him.

We said goodbye, and then it was just the three of us.

"I don't know about you, but I think I'm glad snow is heading in," Kai said as he put away groceries.

"Yeah?"

"We can pretend we're snowed in. Nowhere to go, nothing to do except make Christmas cookies and crafts."

I yawned. "That actually sounds amazing."

"Tomorrow. No work, no nothing, unless it involves being lazy and making memories."

My heart caught in my throat. I should bring up finding my own place. I should tell him how much I appreciated his kindness and generosity, but I didn't want to keep cramping his style.

But I couldn't.

I couldn't do it.

My heart screamed at me, begging me not to leave.

Not to take away its other half.

Instead, I swallowed thickly.

"Making memories, huh?" I elbowed him. "Having a baby around has made you sentimental."

"I may only get to do this one time, I wanna get it right," Kai said.

Unable to actually speak, I just nodded.

🍂

"Next year, we're sledding at the park, for sure," Kai said. "Magic and Elsie will have a ball."

We'd woken up to a couple inches of snow. Not enough to truly trap us in the house, but enough to play *snow day* and make Kai's wishes of a lazy day making memories come true.

The whole morning was absolutely perfect. With a fire crackling in the fireplace, and the Christmas lights twinkling, we danced around the kitchen making pancakes and being silly for Elsie.

She squealed in delight every time she saw the Christmas tree, so we turned it into a big game of peek-a-boo. Running in and out of the living room with Elsie, her giggling and reaching for the lights on the tree, one of us jumping out and saying peek-a-boo. The game went on forever until she got fussy and needed a diaper change.

Later, Kai followed a recipe he found on the internet and made a cinnamon mixture to create homemade ornaments. He pressed Elsie's chubby little hand into the heart mold, a perfect indentation of her hand on the ornament.

My heart clenched to think my baby's hand would never again be that small. Next year, she'd be nearing eighteen months old. Heading toward the Terrible Twos, into everything, no longer a baby.

God, parenting sucked. How could you be so excited and proud to see each stage of your child's life come along, yet so sad and scared to watch each stage pass by?

With the entire house smelling of cinnamon, we turned to the cookie baking. The recipe Allison had shared with Kai turned out to be easy and delicious, and he excitedly plated some up for Francis, Blake and Trevor, and Ivy and Emory. Despite how badly we wanted to let Elsie gnaw on a cookie, we decided the sugary treat wasn't something she needed. She happily chewed on a soft piece of mango in the mesh fruit teether and was none the wiser of what she missed out on.

That afternoon we took a brief break from our snow day to funnel through some phone calls while Elsie watched an educational video and got in some tummy time on her mat. Kai and I sat on the couch to do our work, neither of us willing to miss the possibility of her first roll-over. She'd been rocking back and forth for a while, so we were sure the big move was imminent.

By the time the video was over, Elsie had worn herself out and gotten fussy. I'd drawn the short stick and had to make a call neither of us wanted to be involved in. Just as I was greeted by one of our only grumpy clients, Kai finished his call. Eyeing me as Delores started in with demands for the type of place her daughter was looking for, Kai smiled and slapped me on the back.

"I'll get her changed and give her a bottle," he whispered. Picking up a fussy Elsie from where she'd lost interest in her toys, he winked and mouthed, "Good luck." Then he bounced the baby out of the room. "Come on, Else, diaper duty is better than dealing with cranky clients."

I kept one ear on Delores and one ear on Kai as he told Elsie what he was doing as he made her bottle in the kitchen. We'd both taken to helping her language development by telling her all the things we were doing and naming the objects in her little world.

Smiling to myself as Kai's voice trailed away through the house, only to be picked up again by the baby monitor in the bedroom, I clicked through emails from current and prospective clients regarding homes they wished to buy or sell while Delores droned on. She said the same things every time we spoke to her, so taking notes wasn't even necessary these days. But I made sure to interject with words here and there to let her know I was listening. Delores wasn't a lot of fun, but she was a repeat client and we worked hard to keep all our clients happy.

CoJack Realty had been a huge undertaking for two kids fresh out of college, but Kai and I had made it work, and I was damn proud of the name we'd built for ourselves. We were one of the top realty teams in the state, competing easily with some of the bigger names in other states.

Every so often, I'd look at all we'd done, what we'd built—together—and smile. We'd done that. Kai and me. CoJack forever.

Once Delores finally said goodbye, with the promise to call back and check on things in a day or two, I made the executive decision that work was done for the day. After all, it was a day of laziness and making memories.

I clicked over to the parenting blog Kai and I followed. It truly did have questions and answers for almost anything parenting-related. Kai and I shared the account under the name CoJack. I checked for any new tidbits we might find useful. It was a rabbit hole if you let yourself get pulled in.

Instead, I let my mind wander to what Ivy and Trevor had said about Kai and me. What Alicia had recognized the day Kai rescued me—and her words about regretting how she lost Leanna. Francis's story of pain and regret because he didn't tell Sammy how he felt. Dad's words of encouragement—to look at what's right in front of us and take what we deserve.

Would I let myself be happy and in love? Or would I be an old man with painful regrets because I never spoke up?

The baby monitor crackled, and I pictured Kai masterfully taking care of Elsie's diaper and giving her a bottle. The man had picked up on fatherhood like a damn pro. "Okay, clean diaper. Let's eat. And a nap sounds like a great idea, maybe I'll join you," Kai muttered.

Elsie, obviously a bit happier with a dry diaper, cooed her precious baby sounds—some of her babbles had started to sound suspiciously like words in the last week or so—over the monitor and my heart melted. Would I ever *not* turn to goo when it had to do with my daughter?

The baby monitor Kai had picked out truly was top-of-the-line. We hadn't set up the video portion of it yet, but the audio was crisp and clear. I heard him settle himself in the recliner and Elsie's noises quieted as I pictured her grasping the bottle in her chubby little hands.

"Hungry girl, huh?" Kai mused, a smile lacing his words.

I could just imagine him looking down at Elsie with so much wonder and love. His brown hair all messy, strong legs spread and rocking the recliner, hand patting Elsie's diaper-covered rump.

My heart ached.

And then...

"What am I going to do, Else?" A pause and a sigh. "That daddy of yours is driving me insane."

For a moment, my heart stopped. Was Kai tired of having me in his home? Oh god, maybe this situation wasn't working out as well as I'd thought it was. I'd known we'd have to leave, I just wasn't ready.

Shit.

"Do you know how long I've loved him?" A snort of laughter. "I mean really loved him? Twenty-five years I've loved him like a brother. But the for-real, all-consuming, want him any and every way I can get him kind of love?" He blew out a breath, the monitor picking up every sound, and I froze, my heartbeat increasing to Mach ten. "Since I was sixteen, Else. Before that if we're being honest." Another pause, and I pictured Kai running a hand over his face and through his hair while I struggled to breathe. "What am I supposed to do with that? I can't fuck things up—excuse my language; do *not* repeat that word—but keeping this to myself is absolutely killing me. I don't know how much longer I can do it."

Elsie made a grunting noise and Kai laughed with no humor.

"I know, right? Keep it to myself and slowly go insane with how badly I want the man I love and can't have, or tell him and risk losing the other half of my soul? Damned if I do, damned if I don't."

His words had me dizzy.

Or maybe that was a lack of oxygen to my brain.

Kai patted Elsie's back until she burped, and I played statue on the couch.

The recliner creaked and I knew Kai was standing to walk Elsie around until she fell asleep. Then he'd lay her down and leave the bedroom.

This was it. The moment I'd been waiting for since I was eighteen.

I left the living room and headed toward our bedroom.

Toward the first day of the rest of my life.

CHAPTER 11

KAI

GRATEFUL ELSIE WENT DOWN EASILY, I TURNED toward the door intent on rescuing Colby from Delores. The woman wasn't easy, and she could talk a blue streak.

I froze.

Colby stood in the doorway.

How long had he been there? Did he hear me spill my heart to Elsie?

No. I would have seen him standing there.

He shifted and I noticed the monitor in his hand.

The top-of-the-line picks up every single little sound monitor. He had the receiver. The base unit was in the bedroom.

Where I'd told Elsie I was in love with her dad.

With no time to decide how to play the situation, I just put my finger to my lips and walked toward him. Bustling him from the doorway, I closed the door behind me.

I'd play this as normal as possible.

As we neared the living room, Colby grabbed my hand and stopped me.

I looked down at our hands and back up at Colby's face.

Tension laced across his features.

But there was something else.

Something I couldn't quite pin down.

Was he angry? Upset?

Pleased?

"I love you," Colby blurted.

I smiled. Just keep things normal. "I love you too."

Dear god, why was my voice so raspy and high? And were hands supposed to be that sweaty?

Colby stepped closer, pressing my back to the wall. "No, I *love* you. For real. I liked calling you my husband." He rested his forehead against mine. "I like living with you. I like raising our daughter together. I. Love. You."

What in the actual fuck was happening? Had I fallen asleep rocking Elsie and this was all a dream?

My first attempt failed as I struggled to find words. Finally, I cleared my throat. "What do you mean? What are you saying?"

Colby's hand came up to cup my face and he closed his eyes, breathing me in. "I'm saying, I just heard every word you told our daughter."

My breath caught. "I—"

"No, Kai, I need to say this. Fuck." He nuzzled his nose against mine. "I've needed to say this since we were eighteen."

Oh, god.

"I'm listening." Tremors traveled through my body. My heart wanted to shut out the world and just let Colby hold me. My brain blasted *danger, danger*; all my synapses firing, preparing to retreat. What did Colby need to say? How was this going to change my life?

I knew deep in my soul what I wanted him to say, but I also knew that the heart doesn't always get what it most desperately wants.

"Remember the day we made that deal?" Colby asked, his eyes closed, forehead pressed against mine.

I nodded.

"Well, we're thirty and single. I wanna collect on it."

"What?" I rasped out.

"I love you. I've loved you since we were five, but I fell for you for real when I was eighteen. Maybe before."

"But you never…" I whispered.

"You didn't either."

"Touché." I smiled, loving the laugh lines that crinkled Colby's face. "Go on."

"I don't know exactly when it started, but I knew by the time I was eighteen that I wanted to kiss you and hold you and love you in all the ways we hadn't experienced together."

"But you left." My words caught. "How could you love me and leave like that?"

Colby sighed. "The same way my brain is screaming at me right now to take off. Telling me I'm not worth it. I'll just mess things up for you. I don't deserve to be happy and in love."

"That's all the shit with your mom talking." I put my hands on both sides of his face. "None of that is true." I shook his head. "No, look at me. You are worth *everything*. You make my life better just by being in it. You deserve every ounce of happiness and love. Do you hear me?"

Colby grunted, slamming his eyes shut again. "I've wanted to tell you for so long."

"Why didn't you?"

He cracked an eye. "Guess I could ask you the same."

"I asked first." I bumped my hips into his.

Fucking hell.

That was a mistake.

Huge mistake.

Oh god, even the slightest press of my cock against his was enough to have me dying to grip his ass and thrust our bodies together.

Shit.

Shit.

Shit.

Colby had to have noticed it if the way he sucked in air and gritted his teeth was any indication.

Was he as turned on as me?

Put off?

"I always figured you'd tell me if there was something there for you. When you didn't, I convinced myself I was better off loving my best friend and keeping him in my life rather than letting him know I'd fallen in love with him and risk losing the best person I've ever known." Colby took a deep breath. "I'm not fuckin' around, Kai. Life without you wouldn't be worth livin' even if I could get through it on my own. I can't lose you."

Carding my fingers through the soft, silky blond locks at the back of his head, I swallowed thickly before making a frustrated sound and pressing a hard kiss to Colby's forehead. "Fuck, Cole. I get it. I fell for you at thirteen—fuckin' thirteen—I didn't exactly know what it meant, but

I knew I wanted to crawl into your pocket and be with you always."

Colby sniffed.

"And then hormones hit, and I was bombarded with all this shit I wanted to do with you—but even then, it was all very vague and shadowy in my mind—I just knew I wanted to touch you. Kiss you. And jerking off always ended with visions of you no matter how hard I tried to think of *anyone* else."

This time, Colby laughed. "May have had my fair share of the same. Just a little later than you figured things out."

"So, what does this mean? Where does this leave us?" I asked, thrilled and terrified at the same time.

"Like I said, I want to call in that deal. Give us a chance." Colby pulled back, his eyes locking with mine. "If you're on board?"

"Don't be a dumbass, I've loved you forever."

"Is it enough?" Worry passed over Colby's face.

I gripped his hair and pressed my temple to his, bringing my lips to his ear. "What we have will always be enough. We'll figure it out."

Colby gave a shaky laugh. "Will we?"

I pulled back, whispers of doubt wisping through me. "Why wouldn't we?"

He scoffed. "We couldn't even be honest with each other about how we felt. We lost so many years. How can we make something work if we can't even tell the fucking truth?"

I cupped his face and stared deep into those light blue eyes I knew better than my own. "We make it work the same way we've made this friendship work for twenty-five years. By loving each other. Trusting each other. Knowing each other better than we know ourselves."

Colby snorted.

A smirk tugged at my lips. "Okay, we got a little off track in the knowing each other department since neither of us figured this shit out."

"Other people figured it out before we did."

I cocked a brow.

"My neighbor back in California. My dad. Ivy and Trevor."

Laughter bubbled from me. "Emory and Blake too. And Francis."

"What's wrong with us?"

I shook my head, a wash of sorrow dampening the thrill of what Colby and I had finally admitted to each other.

"What?" Colby scowled. "What's wrong?"

"I'm just thinking about all the years we missed out on."

It was Colby's turn to shake his head. "We weren't ready back then. I had too much shit to work through. As badly as I knew I wanted you, I wasn't in a place to make it work." He wrapped an arm around my waist and pulled me close, my lungs freezing. "I needed to grow up, figure some things out. Plus, we wouldn't have Elsie."

"Cole?"

"Yeah?"

"I wanna kiss you so fuckin' bad," I whispered, a million butterflies fluttering in my chest.

"Fuck." Colby tightened his arm around me and brought a hand up to brush knuckles over my cheek. "What if I'm bad at it and mess everything up?"

"Then we practice until we're good at it," I said. "But I'm so fuckin' hard I could pound nails, so I don't think it's gonna suck."

Colby moved to cup the back of my head and pulled me close, his breath feathering over my mouth. "I want this. I want you. I want it all, whatever you can give me."

"You already own every part of me." My lips ghosted over his.

He kissed me. Soft and tentative at first, but then the flame smoldering between us all those years sparked to life, and Colby deepened the kiss. Devouring my mouth in the sweetest, hottest kiss of my life.

His scent wrapped around me, comforting and familiar. The taste of his mouth something new and exciting, promising so much more. Warmth seeped between us, my hips rocking, searching.

It wasn't clear who moaned first, but the whimper as the kiss ended was definitely me.

"Holy shit." Colby huffed, breathing heavily.

"Didn't suck?" I asked with a breathless chuckle.

"Didn't suck at all."

CHAPTER 12

COLBY

"Couch, now." One kiss with Kai would never be enough. Every single fantasy I'd ever had about the man raced through my head, begging to take the spotlight, screaming at me to make things happen before I woke up and Kai was gone.

But he was there. In my arms. Hands and lips exploring, savoring, reaching for promises that stretched before us. We'd started an insatiable inferno, our bodies begging for more.

He grinned and licked his lips. "Bossy."

"We've got very little time before Else wakes up," I warned.

Kai kissed me again. "Good point. Get naked."

"Now who's bossy?" But I yanked my shirt over my head and grabbed the hem of Kai's.

By the time we kissed, stripped, and fumbled our way to the couch, we each had a bundle of clothes and balls about to explode.

Shirts and jeans ended up unceremoniously tossed to

the floor. Laptops slammed shut. Folders and papers shoved from the couch. The baby monitor placed on the corner of the coffee table.

And then we were stretched out, on our sides, facing each other.

"I can't stop touching you," Kai murmured against my neck, his hand roaming up and down my back. "I want to enjoy it, but I'm scared if I don't soak it all up now, you'll disappear."

"We've got time." Dragging my thumb over his lips, I dipped to press our lips together. "Fast, slow, hard, soft," I panted, "whatever you want, I'm here for it."

Kai huffed out a laugh. "Yes, please. All the above. We could hide away for a year, and it still wouldn't be enough for all I want to do with you."

"Sex fiend," I teased.

Kai sobered, shaking his head. "I like sex, it's fun, and I definitely want to explore with you. But this is different. This has my chest hot and about to burst. My heart has never been involved like this before."

Our kiss was long and slow, hot tongues gliding together.

"Maybe that's why it feels so right," I murmured against his lips. "Our hearts were in it long before our bodies."

"Oh, my body was down long ago," Kai teased. "Do you know how many nights I dreamed about touching you? How badly I wanted your hands all over me?"

"Tell me what you dreamed." My husky words brought a shiver from Kai. We both moaned when I rocked my hips, bringing our hard lengths together, only thin layers of cotton between us.

"Me on my knees." Kai grunted when I thrust again. "Swallowing you, taking your load."

"Fuck, Kai." I gripped his ass and pulled him close, wanting our bodies to be one.

"Your mouth on me, hands stroking, getting me off. Never went much further because I usually blew my load before I got to anything else." He rocked, rutting our cocks together. The underwear was definitely in the way.

"I wanna know every single thing you like so I can do it all a million times," I said. "But I'm not gonna last long and I might die if she wakes up before we get off."

Kai snaked an arm between us, shoving his underwear down, the elastic waistband under his balls, his rock-hard cock bobbing between us. "This good?" he asked, his words rough, delicious tension building between us.

My garbled answer made little sense, but he caught my meaning when I mimicked his move, nearly ripping the fabric as I yanked my underwear down to expose my dick.

Kai anchored his arms around me and threw a leg over mine, our precum-slick cocks pressed firmly side-by-side. In a haze, like every wet dream come true, I kissed him and thrust into him. It was too much all at once, and not even close to enough.

"Colby," Kai panted. "Fuck, Cole, I wanna come. Wanna feel you all over me. Fuck. Don't wanna stop."

My body understood his frantic pleas, begging to savor the moment, screaming to explode. "Fuck," I grunted. "Fuck, Kai, I'm close."

He reached between us and took our throbbing cocks in hand. "Give me your hand."

I wrapped my fingers around his, and we stroked. Kai

thumbed over my leaking slit. I did the same. "Oh shit," I moaned.

Our stroking eventually divided, and we jerked each other off. My eyes couldn't pull away from the gorgeous sight of Kai's fist around my dick. The sensation of another cock in my hand was new and exciting; all I wanted to do was make Kai come.

"Fuck, Cole, I'm so close," Kai whimpered.

"Kiss me."

Our lips melded together as our slick fists glided up and down rock-hard shafts.

My balls drew tight moments before my cock erupted between us, cum splattering my belly and dripping down Kai's knuckles. Moaning, Kai thrust hard into my fist, his orgasm exploding, coating my hand.

We lay together, catching our breaths.

I waited for a freak out.

Waited for regret.

For the world to end.

Nothing happened.

A chuckle escaped my lips.

"What?" Kai asked with a satisfied grin.

"That was over embarrassingly fast."

He huffed. "A decade of edging will do that."

I winced as the evidence of our naptime activity cooled between my fingers. "Good thing this couch is easy-to-clean."

Knowing we had to leave our little bubble of bliss, I groaned, leaning in to kiss him. "I wasn't just angling for an orgasm when I said I love you," I whispered against his lips. "I do. I know we've got a lot to figure out—"

Kai shut me up with a kiss. "You love me and I love

you, that's the biggest hurdle and we've already soared over it. We've got this. CoJack forever, don't ever forget."

Elsie's little wake-up noises filled the air. We had about three minutes before she let loose with wails to express her extreme displeasure.

We were dressed and cleaned up in record time.

Walking into our bedroom to get our daughter from her nap was something we'd done about a hundred times.

But that day was different.

That day was a new beginning.

The rest of the day was every bit as normal as ever but also filled with secret smiles, soft brushes of hands, stolen kisses, and giddy anticipation.

Elsie, oblivious that her two favorite people—our only true competition was Magic, if I was being honest—had confessed their love to each other almost a decade after the fact, continued being the most adorable baby in the world.

Two grown men, completely wrapped around a tiny human who hadn't even been on the planet a full three hundred and sixty-five days, stretched out on the floor and made absolute fools of ourselves as we vied for her attention, and stimulated her perfect little brain.

"Oh my god," Kai whispered. "I think she's going to do it." He nodded toward Elsie, who was about half an inch from an actual rollover to her back.

I wanted to help her, wanted to reach out, but Kai took my hand.

"Let her do it. She knows something is supposed to happen. Look how determined she is."

There, in the soft living room light, a faint hue of blue shining on us from the Christmas tree, and the scent of cinnamon hanging on the air, we watched with bated breath as our daughter cooed and rocked.

And rolled over.

We whooped.

She looked shocked, arching her neck to look at us upside down from her new position.

And then she cried.

Kai scrambled to pick her up, patting her back. "Shhhh, it's okay. You're such a big girl, rolling over already." He kissed her head.

Once she'd settled down, Kai put her back down on her tummy.

Elsie, like anyone excited to learn a new skill, rolled about a hundred times. The first few times continued to shock her, and she hadn't figured out how to get herself back to her tummy just yet, but she'd play on her back until she got fussy. Then one of us would turn her back over, and the game would begin again.

"She's a genius," Kai whispered against my lips.

"Obviously," I agreed. "Takes after her dads."

"I know we said there was no real reason for gifts this year since she wouldn't even know what was going on—and our parents will spoil her rotten with a million presents—but…" Kai's eyes sparkled.

"What did you do?" I asked.

"I just got her a couple things…"

"It's fine," I said with a sheepish smile, "I just want to make sure we didn't get duplicates."

Kai beamed. "I got a couple books for bedtime, the sweetest little black dog stuffy—seriously, it looks just like Magic—and this set of sensory balls." He shrugged. "And this walker thing that can turn into a grocery cart or toy stroller when she's older. I asked in the group for ideas. Everything is highly rated for her age, I made sure before buying it."

"God, I love you," I said, leaning close and kissing him. "You are fucking amazing."

Kai blushed and kissed me back. "What did you get her, Mr. No Gifts this Year?"

It was my turn to shrug. "A gigantic caterpillar with a bunch of different sounds and feels on each section, a stacking toy, and bedtime books."

Kai kissed me again. "So, we're good. No duplicates. I might have picked out a couple super cute outfits, too."

I huffed and rolled my eyes.

"What? I got them in bigger sizes for later."

"You're too good to be true." I pressed my forehead to his. "How did we get so lucky?"

"It must be the Christmas magic," Kai quipped with a grin. "The town is brimming with it, you know."

We both laughed.

Elsie made a noise and we turned.

And gasped.

She was up on her hands and knees, rocking forward and back.

"Oh my god," Kai whispered. "She's trying to crawl."

Elsie blew raspberries and rocked some more as if to celebrate her two huge achievements in one day.

My heart hurt.

I loved watching her learn and grow, but every next

step meant my baby was one moment closer to being a toddler, then a child, then a teen, then an adult.

"Hey," Kai murmured against my ear. "You okay?"

I sniffed and swallowed the melancholy. "Yeah, it's just hard to be so excited to see her growing and meeting all these milestones, while not wanting her to grow up at all." Shaking my head, I tried to make sense. "Like, I want to see her in every phase; I'm excited for the future. But I also don't want her to ever change from this exact moment right here."

Elsie's pudgy little arms gave out and she face-planted which effectively ended my little pity party as she screamed her head off.

Then it was dinner, bath time, and books. Elsie ate like a champ, squealed as if her bath was the best thing ever, and babbled while patting every page of each book we read to her.

Then it was time for a bottle and bed. She sucked down the bottle, but as if recognizing a major shift—her own big day of milestones along with Kai and me—and not wanting to miss out on the fun, Elsie fought bedtime like a boss.

Once she finally gave in, Kai and I collapsed on the couch.

"What are you thinking?" I asked, manhandling him until we were cuddled together on the far end.

The living room was dark except for the glow from the tree. Kai's eyes sparkled. "A million and one things. Is it okay to have sex with a baby in our room? How quickly can I get a bed in one of the upstairs bedrooms? Can our parents watch Elsie for a night so we can fuck each other's brains out?" He caught my hand as it trailed up and down his arm. "And when am I going to wake up and realize this is all a dream?"

"All valid," I teased. "Pretty sure siblings wouldn't exist in such high numbers if sex with a baby in the same room wasn't something that happens. But let's order a bed tomorrow."

We both chuckled.

"I'm down with asking our parents to babysit," I said. "And I get the feeling of thinking we're going to wake up and find out it's not real."

Kai turned in my arms and pressed a kiss to my lips. "What else? I can see shit in your eyes, Cole. What's up? Too much too fast?"

I scoffed. "Too fast? It's taken us over a decade."

He smirked and ran a hand over my chest. After so many years of keeping things platonic, we were both unable and unwilling to keep our hands to ourselves. Our earlier confessions were like permission to touch, and we soaked in every single chance we got.

"Okay, so what's got that worry line digging so deep?" Kai traced a finger between my brows. "Being bi? Coming out? We can take things slowly if you need to."

I shoved him gently, catching him with a laugh before he tumbled off the couch. "Fuck that, you know that shit doesn't bother me. Maybe if I was trying to start something with another guy, but not with you."

"Okay, okay." Kai's hand glided down my arm and laced our fingers together. "Talk to me. We can make this work, but we have to be honest."

Ignoring his words for a moment, I pulled him close and captured his mouth. God, did anything in the world taste better than Kai's kiss? The press of his lips against mine, the slick heat of our tongues. Our bodies melted together as the kiss heated up.

"Nope." Kai broke the kiss, gasping. "As badly as I want to forget the world and just spend days making out, we can't. For one, we have a baby and jobs. Two, we can't cover shit up. Now, talk to me."

"I want this more than anything, but I'd give it all up if that was the only way to keep you as a friend." The words rushed out of me.

Kai's face softened and he cupped my cheek. "It's not an either-or situation. We can have this and keep our friendship."

"What if we can't? What if trying to add sex and romance fucks things up and we can't survive?"

He shook his head. "No way. We've survived a lot of shit over the years. This friendship isn't flimsy."

I rolled my eyes. "We haven't survived the fallout of me sticking my dick in you and hoping everything can just stay normal."

Kai laughed so loud I worried Elsie would wake up.

I slapped a hand over his mouth. The nip of his teeth against my palm sent fire through my blood.

Kai rocked his hips against me. "We're going to revisit the whole dick-sticking conversation," he whispered, feathering his lips over mine. "But let's focus. *As I was saying...*" Kai nuzzled his nose to mine. "We've survived a lot. True, maybe most of it didn't involve our dicks, but we have a strong friendship. Remember when you flushed my carnival goldfish?"

I snorted. "Oh god, it was floating. I thought it was dead."

"Little fucker perked right up in the toilet, but it was

too late." Kai squeezed my hand. "And when you lost my most valuable Pokémon card? That was a true test of friendship."

"Damn, I never did figure out where that thing went. I think that little shit Marvin stole it when I took it to school." I lost myself in Kai's hazel eyes. Was this real? I'd wanted him for so long, and now we were cuddled on the couch as if we'd been a couple forever. Well, in reality, we kinda had. Just without the sex and romance. And now we had it all. "What about the five thousand times you wrecked my bike?"

"And when you made the soccer team, but I didn't?" Kai smiled at the memory.

"I quit the team for you."

"You said you quit the team because the coach was an asshole."

I shrugged. "Same difference."

"Ohhhh, do you remember when you flooded the bathroom, but you let me take the blame? That was a close call. I was grounded over that."

Wincing, I rested my hand on Kai's hip. "Yeah, that one was shitty." I kissed his cheek. "Sorry."

"And when Carmen Delgado was blowing both of us behind our backs, but when she got caught, she said she liked you best? That was rough."

I couldn't help but laugh. "Oh god, we were such shits back then."

"What about when you let me drive your car, even though you'd been told not to, and I wrecked it into the bushes? You told your dad *you* had jumped the curb."

A tight warmth spread through my chest. "I guess we've made it through a lot of shit, huh?"

Kai kissed me. "We survived *all* that plus you moving away, getting married and divorced, and having a baby. Twenty-five years is solid, man. It doesn't dissolve in an instant."

"I want this," I said against his lips, "but I'm also terrified we'll give it a shot and make things weird. What if we can't come back from it and everything is ruined?

Kai shook his head. "We've showered together—not like either of us is going to be surprised by anything. Even before today, I've seen your dick. We're just going to get a little more up close and personal." He locked eyes with me and fought the smile teasing his lips. "Plus, I already know how bad you can blow up a bathroom—*that* is grounds for terminating a friendship if ever there was one. And I haven't killed you for the god-awful snoring. Yet. We've got this."

My heart nearly thudded out of my chest. "CoJack forever?"

"Forever."

CHAPTER 13

KAI

"OH. MY. GOD." EMORY SQUEALED AS HE LED THE group into our kitchen the next day. Throwing his arms around me, he danced me around the room. "You told him?"

Ivy, Trevor, and Blake smirked and slapped Colby on the back.

"Told me what?" Colby asked, an attempt at a scowl on his gorgeous face. "What's going on? Kai?"

Emory froze.

The other three's eyes went wide.

I shrugged and Colby crossed his arms over his chest, the only sound in the room was Elsie's babble as she reached pudgy little hands for Magic as he sat next to her highchair.

Emory's eyes went back and forth between Colby and me, and he pursed his lips. "Nope. I'm not buying it. Something definitely changed between the two of you."

Ivy draped his arms over Emory's shoulders. "Still looks like a lot of pent-up sexual tension to me, Em."

Emory shook his head. "No. I mean, yes. That's still there but *look* at them. They're different." He turned to Trevor and Blake. "You guys see it, right?"

My cheeks burned and I thought of what Colby and I had gotten up to in the shower before bed, and again this morning when we'd gotten handsy before Elsie woke up.

"Sorry," Blake said with a grin. "You two definitely look guilty."

Emory shoved his glasses up his nose. "Please," he begged, his palms pressed together, "please tell me you put each other out of your misery and admitted you're madly in love."

All four men stared at us. I wanted to scream from the rooftops that Colby and I had finally pulled our heads from our asses and took things to the *more than friends* stage, but I didn't want to overstep if Colby wasn't ready.

I'd never known him to worry about what anyone thought of him, and he'd taken my bisexuality in stride—been my biggest supporter, actually—but it wasn't my place to out him if he wasn't ready.

Colby huffed a chuckle and threw an arm over my shoulder. "When we were eighteen, we made a deal that if we were single at thirty, we'd give in and give us a shot since everyone already thought we were together anyway." He kissed my cheek. "And I might have finally grown the balls to tell him I love him."

Emory whooped so loud that Magic barked, and Elsie cried.

"Way to go, Em, make the baby cry," Ivy teased.

Emory rushed to pick Elsie up, singing and dancing her around the kitchen, dodging Magic as he shoved his nose into Emory's leg, his tail whacking everything in sight. When Elsie giggled through her tears, Emory kissed her head and handed her over to Ivy.

The dark, inked-up, broody man looked as if he'd been handed a bomb with a ten-second timer. But Elsie patted his face, blew a raspberry, and squirmed until she could see the dog again.

"Want me to take her?" Colby asked.

Ivy blushed but bounced Elsie a bit. When she giggled, he shook his head. "She's fine."

Colby, Trevor, and Ivy headed outside a bit later—Elsie had finally grown tired of blowing raspberries at Ivy—to grill veggies and burgers for lunch.

Blake made his way between the kitchen and the patio like a kid who couldn't stand to be left out of either conversation.

Emory hugged me again as we set the table. "I'm so happy for you. Tell me all the details."

I filled him in on my confession to Elsie caught on the baby monitor.

Emory covered his mouth in glee.

"Then he grabbed my hand and told me he loved me," I said. "I told him I loved him too. He was like, 'No, I *love* you. I liked calling you my husband at the hospital.'"

Emory's glasses almost fell from the tip of his nose in his excitement, but he shoved them back in place. "What?! His husband?"

So, I had to tell that story too.

By the time the guys came in with lunch, Emory's eyes were sparkling and he bounced with energy.

"Damn, you let him get into the sugar?" Ivy asked, hauling Emory against his chest, the younger man's back pressed to Ivy's front.

Emory sighed, tipping his head back for a kiss. "Kai was just telling me a love story and it's got me all up in my feels."

Colby hooked an arm around my waist and yanked me close. "Better be *our* love story or I might have to get jealous," he murmured against my ear before kissing my cheek.

Emory sighed again. "Oh my god, aren't they the sweetest?"

Ivy cleared his throat. Blake chuckled. Trevor pretended to gag.

We bustled around the kitchen, filling plates, pouring wine, getting Elsie's lunch ready, and giving each other a hard time like friends and family do.

God, I loved it.

I had fabulous parents.

My best friend—boyfriend? Was that what we were now?—was amazing.

But having a group of friends I thought of as family was something I'd been missing in my life.

A knock on the door silenced our chatter. I headed toward the door as the rest of the crew settled at the dining room table.

Francis stood in the cold, light snowflakes pelting him. "I don't want to intrude," he started.

I swung the door open. "Get in here before you freeze. We're just now eating, can you stay?" The older man could be a total drama queen, and he was sure to spread any bit of gossip from one end of Peppermint Hollow to another, but my heart seemed unable to be anything but fond of him.

"I shouldn't," he hedged.

"Please, stay. Everyone's here and there's plenty of food." I guided him toward the dining room. "Look who I found."

Magic came to inspect the new arrival, and all the guys welcomed Francis to the table. When I returned from the kitchen with a plate full of food and a glass of wine, Francis thanked me profusely. "I'm so sorry to show up empty-handed. How rude of me. I just wanted to pop in to let you know I'll be gone for a bit, visiting my great niece in Wyoming."

I took my seat next to Colby. "That sounds like a nice trip. What part of Wyoming?" I took a sip of my wine, just trying to make friendly small talk.

Francis started to answer, but when he caught sight of Colby's hand moving to my thigh, he froze. "Forget Wyoming. Does this mean what I think it means?"

My cheeks were on fire, but I nodded. "Gonna give it a go."

Colby kissed my cheek and bumped his shoulder into mine.

Francis held a hand to his neck and shook his head. "This is the most lovely news. Truly a Christmas wish come true."

"Your story about Sammy stuck with me," Colby said. "Didn't want to find myself regretting anything years from now."

Francis wiped a tear. "I love that. Knowing our heartache brought about something good, makes it a little easier to bear."

By the time we'd cleaned up the kitchen and said our goodbyes, Elsie was more than ready for her nap. She cried when Magic left, but a quick diaper change and a bottle calmed her quickly, and she went down easily.

"We could nap while she does," Colby whispered in my ear. "Couple blankets on the floor in the spare room, play around for a bit, snuggle up until she wakes up. We've got company coming tonight, better rest up."

Which was how we found ourselves scurrying to spread out blankets in the guest room, rushing through a quick shower in the hall bathroom, and giggling like horny teens as we toppled to the floor on our makeshift pallet.

Warm, naked bodies, exploring hands, lips and tongues savoring.

Colby broke away. "I used to hate when you'd talk about sex with people you dated—"

I snorted. "Same."

"But god," he murmured into my neck, nuzzling the sensitive skin under my jaw. "I wish I'd paid attention. I want to know everything about what you like."

I shook my head. "We'll learn each other together. What do you want to know?"

"Do you like to top or bottom?" Colby's cheeks burned pink, but the flare of desire in his eyes sent a shiver of anticipation through me.

"I'm vers. Truly." I ran my hand up and down Colby's back. Would I ever get used to the fact I could touch him the way I'd longed to for so many years? "I've had great sex with people who bottomed for me, people who topped me, it just depends on the vibe and what all parties want."

"*All* parties?" Colby asked, eyes wide. "You never told me about threesomes."

I shrugged. "Never had any. Not against them, just not

really for me. Bisexuality—when it's not being erased or labeled as *can't make up your mind*—seems to be seen as greedy and wanting multiple partners. Again, not against anyone who wants that, but it's just not me. If I were to have ever gotten involved with two or more people, I would have wanted it to be an actual relationship, not just sex, and I didn't see myself ever being able to commit to anything." My chest fluttered. "I was kinda hung up on this guy…"

Colby smiled. "Hmmm, that whole hang up thing is probably why my two attempted relationships didn't work out."

I cocked a brow and smirked.

He buried his head in my shoulder. "That and the fact they were both addicts with more issues than lifeboats on the Titanic."

"There weren't that many lifeboats on the Titanic; that was part of the problem."

"Oh my god, shut up. My *point* is that I couldn't make anything work with anyone else because of what I felt for you." He rolled his eyes. "And some other reasons, but those are crappy and I'd rather focus on you."

Leaning in, I gripped his chin and kissed him. The taste of him on my lips was my new favorite flavor. "What about what you like?" Bringing us back to the original topic when we finally broke apart. "You like butt stuff?" I kept the words teasing like I would have if we were still in our just friends era.

Colby swallowed and his gaze bore into mine. "I've played around a bit."

Fuck.

I hadn't expected that.

"Did you like it?" My husky words scraped out like a prayer.

He shrugged. "Like you said, depends on the vibe and that wasn't it back then." He rocked his hips into me. "But this is different; I want to do it all."

It was my turn to swallow thickly. "What's *all*?"

"I'm not against kinky stuff, just not my go-to usually. But I want to do everything with you. Stuff I've done, stuff I haven't done."

"Like…" I pressed. I wanted *everything* with Colby too, but I wanted us to be on the same page.

"Blow jobs, rimming, fingers, anal to start with." He nibbled on my collarbone. "Toys? Cuffs? Really, anything. I'm so fuckin' turned on right now, I can't even think of other shit."

"Sounding? Fisting?" I offered.

Colby's eyes went wide. "Okay, maybe not that. I'm not judging anyone who is into it, but it's a bit much for me. Scat, blood, that kind of stuff is probably out—but with you, I'd never say never."

Holy fuck.

"Is that the type of stuff you like?" Colby hedged.

I laughed. "No. If you were expecting any of that, I'll be a very vanilla disappointment."

Colby shook his head and chuckled. "Damn, I was thinking I did a shit job of listening when you talked about sex if you were into that." He sucked gently on my neck. "We've got over a decade to make up for, we'll be plenty busy. Vanilla or not."

"So, do you think you're top-only?"

He ran a thumb over my nipple. When I moaned, he dipped to suck the tight bud between his lips, swirling his tongue over it and blowing softly. I shivered and whimpered, rolling my hips in search of friction.

"No, I don't think I'm top-only. At least not with you."

My world whited out.

I cleared my throat. "You want to bottom?"

Colby nodded. "I want to fuck you so bad, but I want to know what it feels like to have a dick sliding into my ass, so I want to bottom first." He kissed me, biting my bottom lip softly, sucking the stinging flesh until I gripped his ass. "And when I'm fucking you, I want to feel your cum dripping from my ass."

Holy.

Fucking.

Shit.

I thrust my hips hard, bringing our cocks together. "Fuck, Cole, I wanna taste you."

"Can I go first?" Colby asked.

"Really? You wanna suck me off?" I was horny as hell, but I pulled back enough to study his face. "For real?"

Colby nodded. "I want to do it. Been wanting to do it. But I may be *really* bad, so I'd rather go first and not have to follow some stellar cock-sucker extraordinaire."

Laughing, I buried my face in his shoulder. "I'm not gonna turn down the chance to see my dick between your lips—been dreaming of that for over ten years—but I promise you anything that involves your mouth anywhere near my balls will *forever* be fucking fantastic."

"Does sex bring out your alliterative side?" Colby teased, his hand trailing down my chest, fingers brushing over the path of hair from my midsection to my dick.

"Shut up and get busy. We're on the clock."

Eyes bright, Colby brought his lips to mine. "So fucking

sexy." His whispered words pulled a whimper from me and I rocked my hips into his. "Can you stand against the wall?"

My eyeballs were seriously going to fall out of their sockets if he kept dropping bombs on me. "For real?"

Colby shrugged. "It's just how I pictured it and want to do it that way the first time."

I stood and pressed my back against the cool wood door, spreading my legs. "You been picturing anything else?"

"Blowing you like this, fucking you bent over the couch—maybe on the kitchen counter—sixty-nine with two dicks sounds fun, bunch of different positions, in the shower..." Colby listed each item as he knee-walked over to kneel in front of me.

"Fuck, I'm gonna die, but at least I'll do it knowing my dreams came true." My head thunked against the door as Colby nuzzled my lower abdomen, pressing kisses along the sensitive skin. When his hand came up to cup my balls and he swirled his tongue around my cock head, I fought to stay upright.

As much as I wanted to close my eyes and sink into the sensation of his warm, wet mouth around my dick, I couldn't pass up the chance to watch the man of my dreams swallow me down.

Glancing down, my entire world fizzled into meltdown mode. A mixture of absolute perfection swirled with everything I'd ever known coming to a crashing halt. The scene before me was a dream come true, but also the most surreal experience of my entire life.

Colby.

On his knees.

Hands on my hips, fingers digging into my ass, thumbs feathering over my hip bones.

Colby.

Licking his lips.

Looking up at me with those big blue eyes—determination overtaking any unsureness.

He took me between his lips, the smooth heat of his mouth pulling a whimper from me. My hands frantically grasped for something, anything to hold onto as an inferno washed over me.

Lust.

Longing.

But more than anything *love*.

Love for this man I'd known my entire life.

Love for Colby as my soulmate and best friend, Elsie's daddy, and the man I planned to spend the rest of my life with.

"Oh my god," I whispered. With my shoulders pressed to the door, my neck craned to watch, I slowly rocked my hips. Colby let me set a gentle rhythm, big eyes staring up at me, his hands alternating between caressing and gripping my thighs and ass. Reminding myself he was new to sucking cock, I feathered my hand over his soft blond locks.

Fiery desire lit Colby's eyes and his moan vibrated around my dick. Message received loud and clear. Fisting his hair, I increased the speed of my thrusts. He moaned again, gliding his hands from my ass, around and up to my chest. The strong grip of his hands on my pecs went straight to my balls, and the brush of his thumbs over my nipples nearly sent me over the edge.

"Fuck." I grunted and fucked his mouth harder. "Colby, I'm close," I warned.

The pure proud satisfaction in his eyes was one hundred percent Colby. He'd faced a challenge with desire and determination and conquered it. He gripped my ass again and teased a finger between my ass cheeks, barely brushing over my hole.

"Fuck," I mumbled again. "Fuck, so close. Pull off if you don't want it."

Colby shook his head, my spit-slick cock slipping in and out of his mouth.

Unable to hold back any longer, I gave one final thrust and exploded.

For a cock-sucking novice, Colby handled my load surprisingly well. The bit that dribbled down his chin did crazy things to me, but he wiped his mouth and scrambled to the blanket before I could kneel in front of him and kiss my cum from his lips.

Colby fisted his cock and hissed. "Fuck, Kai. I want you to suck me off so bad, but I'm about to fucking blow. Fuuuuck…"

"Do you remember our eighth-grade literature teacher?"

Colby's eyes flew open. "What?"

I shrugged. "Just thought it might help. Remember how she wore those super low-cut shirts that showed her cleavage? Would have been hot as hell, but she was like ninety and had the worst smoker's breath." I chuckled, getting into the memory. "Oh god, her lips were so puckered, and she wore that bright red lipstick."

"Fuck, man," Colby grumbled. "Major boner killer."

I waggled my brows. "Yeah, but now I get to suck you off and finger fuck you before you nut."

"Well-played," Colby said with a sigh, throwing an arm over his eyes. "But now I'm thinking of Mrs. Pettee and it's killing the vibe."

I dropped down onto the blanket and stretched next to him. Capturing his lips, savoring the mix of our flavors, I kissed him long and slow. "You won't be thinking about anything except coming down my throat pretty soon."

Colby grunted, wrapping me in his arms and kissing me within an inch of my life. "Suck me," he murmured against my lips.

For the millionth time since Colby told me he loved me, my brain short-circuited trying to comprehend the words. The situation. Attempting to understand that it was all real. The man I'd loved since I was five, the man I'd wanted something more with before I could even fathom what *more* might be, was kissing me.

Holding me.

Asking me to blow him.

It wasn't a dream.

Wasn't one of my decades-long fantasies.

He loved me back.

Pressing kisses to his jaw, his neck, his collarbone, I paused long enough to nip and suck on his nipples. The roll of Colby's hips combined with the hiss of pleasure meant we'd definitely be revisiting that erogenous zone.

Nuzzling the blond hair on his abdomen, trailing my lips over his naval, I made my way to my prize. Don't get me wrong, I'd marry the man tomorrow even if he said he never wanted to have sex, but knowing he wanted me as much as I wanted him—as evident by his leaking cock and the way he chanted my name like a prayer—was enough to have me drooling in anticipation of tasting him.

I knew his scent. Knew what he smelled like when he was sweaty from working out. Would recognize the clean rush of his soap after a shower anywhere. Had secretly breathed him in during a thousand different hugs and wrestling matches.

But burying my nose in the neatly trimmed thatch of hair at the base of his cock held something new. Soap, sweat, and the very essence of Colby tickled my senses. Groaning, drawing in a deep breath, wanting to savor his scent forever, I cupped his balls.

Colby swore and arched. "Please, Kai." His plea echoed through the room.

Wanting to have some fun before he lost it, I swirled my tongue over his slit, moaning at the flavor of his precum, and took his hard cock between my lips. Bobbing my head up and down, relishing his taste on my tongue, the mix of grunts and whimpers escaping his lips, and the heavy thickness of his length, I nudged his legs apart.

"You want my finger?" Pulling off his cock just long enough to whisper the words and slick my finger with spit.

Colby moaned.

"Words, Cole. Do you want my finger in your ass?"

"Fuck, yeah. Kai, fuck. Please."

"Let me get some lube—"

"No, just give it to me. I want you in me when I come."

Fire exploded in my veins.

"Spread your legs. Roll toward me."

Colby followed directions beautifully.

"Put this leg over me," I coaxed, caressing my hand over his top leg.

The new position kept me right at cock-level and opened Colby up to my touch. Adding extra spit to my finger, I took his cock back between my lips and pressed the spit-slick digit between his ass cheeks. Smearing spit over his hole, I hollowed out my cheeks as I sucked him deep.

I wanted to prop Colby's ass up and feast on him until he was a wet, sloppy mess. But his balls were so tight, I knew he wouldn't last.

We had time.

Instead, I tapped gently against his pucker and pressed in slightly.

Colby moaned and rocked his hips.

Gathering more spit, I slicked his hole again and pressed in deeper.

"Fuck, Kai. I want to feel you inside me. Wanna blow down your throat while you finger my ass."

His words had me moving too quickly, pressing too deep, savoring his cry of ecstasy too much when my finger slipped past his tight ring of muscle. "Shit. Sorry. Too much?" I started to withdraw my finger, but Colby clutched his ass around me.

"No, it's good. Give me another and make me come."

Maneuvering somewhat awkwardly, I brushed a kiss over his balls and spat at the juncture of his hole and my finger. With the extra moisture, I worked a second finger into him and returned to sucking his dick. I wasn't going super deep into his ass—not without lube and not when he'd said he wanted to bottom before he topped me, no need to risk hurting him—but the sensation of having slick fingers in his ass and a warm, wet mouth around his cock was enough to have Colby writhing against me. His leg tightened around my shoulders, and he thrust his hips back and forth between my fingers and my mouth.

I reached up and pinched a nipple with my free hand, teasing over the hard nub before slapping my hand over his pec and gripping hard.

Colby grunted, fisted my hair, buried his cock in my throat, and exploded. The taste of his cum filled my mouth, pumping over my tongue, flowing down my throat. I hummed around his pulsing cock as the orgasm washed over him, my fingers held firmly by the tight ring of his ass.

When he shuddered, whimpering as he rolled slightly away, I had one terrifying moment of fear. Would he regret what we'd done? Had I pushed too far?

Before the worries could take root, Colby grabbed my arm and yanked me on top of him, face-to-face. With both hands buried in my hair, he pulled me into a long, slow, deliciously nasty kiss. Our tongues, still slick and tasting of each other's cum, plunged deep, savoring and offering promises of what was yet to come.

"Was that okay?" I asked. "You're good? It wasn't too much?"

Colby nodded, pressing our foreheads together. "Sex with women is great, not gonna say it's not. But holy fuck, sex with your best friend? Ten out of fucking ten."

I chuckled. "Not sure *all* best friends can say that." I kissed his nose. "But I would give the same review."

We came down from our high as we snuggled close, dozing off and on in our post-orgasmic bliss.

Elsie's cries broke through the silence and we both groaned.

I loved every second of life with Colby and Elsie, but a guy could use a nap after fucking around with the man of his dreams. Real sex was a lot more exhausting than getting off in your fantasies.

But our daughter wasn't going to wait.

Christmas was just around the corner—Emory had a countdown going in the group text and a chain of paper rings hanging from a doorway at the Old Christmas House just in case any of us forgot—and we'd invited our parents over for brunch.

"We're going to tell them, right?" I asked. "If you're not ready, we can wait."

Colby shook his head as we cuddled on the couch while Elsie cooed and batted at a toy. "No, I want to tell them. Hell, my dad was the one giving me shit the other day for not being honest and giving us a chance. He'll be thrilled."

We'd spent the last several days since declaring our love for each other making very creative use of Elsie's nap time, heading to the guest room once she was down for the night, and conserving water with shared showers every morning and evening.

Between the two of us and everything we wanted to do to each other, we never ran out of ideas and easily fell asleep every night thoroughly sexed and knowing we were loved.

Blow jobs, rimming, and fingering, combined with

cuddles, caresses, and kisses had allowed us to learn each other's bodies. We'd shared our fantasies, discussed the best ways to prepare for anal activities—Colby adorably took this learning very seriously and wanted to do it just right—and taken a quick road trip after lunch one day to get tested at a nearby clinic in a bigger town.

When we finally had time to devote to a whole night with no worries about bottles and diapers, I had every intention of spending hours upon hours making love with Colby. With negative tests—I hadn't realized just how concerned Colby had been until tears shone in his eyes as he read his results—we'd opted to go without condoms.

With brunch ready and just waiting for our guests to arrive, Colby and I spent several quiet moments making out on the couch. Stopping every now and then to peek at Elsie, committing the image of her big eyes sparkling in the glittering lights of the Christmas tree, we savored each other, our home, and our family.

Ten minutes before we expected our guests, Colby groaned. "We need to get her diaper changed and nicer clothes on."

I snorted. "Yeah, better get her dressed up so she can puke, smear food, or shit all over her nice outfit."

Colby laughed and caught me in a headlock. The wrestling turned into kissing. Which turned into me on my back, legs spread wide, groaning as Colby rocked his dick against mine. What? We had several years to make up for.

The doorbell rang.

"Fuck," Colby muttered against my lips. "I can't open the door with a boner."

"Well, looks like we're doing just that." I slapped his ass and pushed him off the couch.

We both adjusted our traitorous dicks; secrets, laughter, and fire glowing in our eyes. Colby grabbed Elsie and swung her up in the air, her baby giggles filling the room, and we made our way to the door.

A wash of gratefulness blanketed me, heavy and warm like the scent of cinnamon and pine wrapping around our home. Mom, Dad, Tom, and Allison stood on the front stoop, grinning ear-to-ear, ready to drop absolutely everything and spend time with Elsie. All because Tom and Colby had been given a second chance, my parents loved my best friend as if he were their own, and we'd been blessed with great families—even if the beginning had been rough for Colby.

As with every time I thought of Colby's shitty childhood with his mom, I wanted to ease the pain of his past, but I also knew Colby was the man I loved despite what he'd gone through. His past had made him who he was, and I wouldn't change that. Sure, I'd rather he didn't have the demons his mom left him with, but I loved him exactly the way he was.

Mom swooped in and took Elsie as the whole group kicked off their shoes and made their way to the living room.

"She needs a diaper change," Colby said. "And we didn't get her into nicer clothes yet." He dipped his head sheepishly, cheeks pinking.

My dick threatened to get back in the game at the thought of what had kept us from changing Elsie's clothes, and I cleared my throat to cover up the smile.

Several things happened at once.

Mom gasped, turned to Allison, and they both squealed.

Dad chuckled and rolled his eyes.

Tom mumbled, "About damn time," and slapped Dad on the back.

"Uhhh..." I said.

The four of them schooled their features, Elsie the only one still making silly noises. "Sorry," Mom said, biting back a smile. "Did you boys want to tell us something?"

I narrowed my eyes.

Colby cocked his head.

"How can you tell?" I asked when I realized they all knew something was up between Colby and me.

They all laughed.

"Well," Tom started. "I was a bit late to the game, but I saw it even back in high school. When I met Allison, she immediately thought you two were together. I brought it up to Eric..." He trailed off, gesturing toward my dad.

Dad shrugged. "Your mom and I have had a bet going since you boys were about sixteen."

"What?" I croaked. "What kind of bet?"

Mom bounced Elsie on her hip. "About when you'd finally get together. Your dad thought it would be sooner. I knew just how oblivious guys can be sometimes, so I went with later. We let Tom and Allison in on it years ago."

Colby's eyes went wide. "Is that why you brought it up the other day? Is your guess coming soon?"

Tom blushed. "No, I was with Lacy as far as timing. I thought you'd come home after Florida and Mandy. Allison was the one who said you guys would probably need a push if anything was ever going to happen."

Allison beamed and did a little wiggle dance. "I like winning but seeing you two finally together is the best part."

"Unbelievable," Colby muttered.

"Maybe could have let us in on things years ago." Pouting wasn't very becoming, but it felt right for a situation when your entire family is in on a secret and leaves you out.

"Years ago wouldn't have been the right timing," Mom said with a shrug. "We didn't keep it from you to hurt you."

"Just like Tom had to go through some shit to get to this point in his life," Dad said, giving his friend a gentle, understanding look, "and your mom and I went through years of infertility before having you." He slapped me on the back. "Sometimes, we don't understand the timing of things—think we know a lot better and can move things along a lot faster—but a lot of times, things work out best in the end."

Allison snuggled into Tom's side. "And then we look back on the struggles and realize every moment was getting us ready to be the people we are now."

Tom cleared his throat. "Sorry for pushing the other day. I probably should have left things well enough alone, but I lost patience watching you two get starry-eyed over each other with your heads up your asses."

Colby coughed. "Well, this has been touching, but I'm starving."

Elsie got a diaper change and a comfy outfit.

We ate and laughed over brunch.

Elsie got another diaper change and a new outfit because she spit peas all over the first one.

Then six grown-ass adults sat around the living room oohing and ahhing over Elsie as she rolled, rocked on her hands and knees, kicked her feet, batted at toys, chewed on everything she could get her hands on, and squealed adorably. Outside observers would have thought we'd never seen a baby before.

But come on, this particular baby was above and beyond.

For real.

"Have you given any thought to setting up the baby's room?" Mom hedged while Dad pretended to eat Elsie's belly.

"We like having her close by," Colby said.

"Babies need to have their own space," Mom said gently. "And you have that monitor. You'd hear every little peep."

I shrugged. "We've been talking about getting the guest room and Elsie's room set up. But we're not in any hurry, we'll do it when it feels right."

Colby gave my shoulder an appreciative bump. "Maybe once we get her a room of her own, she can start napping in there to get used to it before moving to overnights."

"That's a great plan," Allison said.

Mom clapped her hands together. "Oh! I just had the best idea!"

I narrowed my eyes. "What?"

"Your dad and I will stay here tonight so Elsie is comfortable in her own space. You boys take a night away —parents need to take care of themselves so they can be at their best for their children."

I didn't hate the idea, but I glanced at Colby. He'd never been away from his daughter.

He scowled and pursed his lips. "I don't know…"

"You can call any time," Mom went on. "I hate to say it, but she likely won't even know you're gone. She's not gotten to that clingy stage just yet. You can leave us with a mile-long list of directions."

"Baby steps," Allison interjected, "but we'll offer a second night. She'll have the best time with her grandparents. We all *did* survive raising children."

Tom cleared his throat and looked sheepish. "Second time's a charm."

I leaned into Colby. "What do you say?"

He shrugged. "I feel guilty leaving her…" he hedged. "But you're right, she's not at a stage where she knows we're even gone yet."

"And when she *does* get to that stage," Mom interrupted, "you'll still need to take care of yourselves. We'll cross that bridge when we get there." She waved her hands in a shooing motion. "Go, go on. Look at that cute little rental just beyond the highway. If they're booked, there's that adorable little motel the next town over; they always decorate so nice for Christmas."

Colby and I moved to the couch and pulled out his laptop while the others played with Elsie. Within two minutes, we'd found the rental Mom talked about. The pictures indicated the home would be decked out for the holidays at this time of the year.

"That reminds me of the Winter Ball. Senior year." I pointed at a tree in the living room decorated in peppermint swirls and candy canes.

"It's not booked," Colby said, biting his lip.

I wondered if he was as anxious to get a whole night alone as I was. "It's your call, I'm good either way."

"They have a deal for buy one night, get the next night half off." Colby turned those big blue eyes my way. "Let's do it."

"Yeah?"

"Our parents will be here the whole time." He nodded toward the four adults on the floor pretending not to strain to hear our conversation. "She adores them. Two whole days and nights, just us."

My heart nearly thumped out of my chest, and I tried to smother a smile. "Let's do it."

We packed quickly, knowing we'd likely be in bed most of the little getaway, and headed toward the door. Colby's anxiety showed in his eyes, but he gave my hand a squeeze once he wrote down directions for bottles, bath, and bedtime. We bombarded our parents with last-minute suggestions and reminders until my mom patted me on the cheek. "We've got this. You can call every hour if you're not too busy. Enjoy your time away. We'll take pictures and video."

"Oh my god, what if she starts crawling while we're gone?" Colby asked.

Mom shook her head. "She's trying, but she's not close yet. If it looks like she's going to, we'll record it. Promise."

Colby took a deep breath and nodded.

Elsie gave sloppy kisses and returned to the peek-a-boo game she and my dad were playing as she ate a snack in her highchair.

"Glad she's so concerned," Colby muttered.

Allison hugged us both. "She'll be making you feel guilty with crocodile tears when you leave soon enough. Enjoy this."

And then we were out the door and piling into Colby's truck. As we pulled out of the driveway, I pointed toward the Old Christmas House. The guys were walking out the door. "Pull over so we can let them know what's up."

Colby maneuvered the truck down the little street between our homes.

Emory pushed his glasses up his nose and hauled himself up on the running board as Ivy chuckled. "You are such a child."

Emory smiled. "What? It's fun, and this truck is sexy."

Trevor shook his head and Blake grinned.

"We're heading to my parents' place for early Christmas. What about you?" Emory asked.

"Our parents are staying with Elsie," I said.

Emory's eyes grew wide. "Where are you going?"

Colby cleared his throat, and I knew his cheeks would be on fire if I looked his way.

"Taking a couple nights away. We'll be back in time for our Christmas lunch."

"Ohhhh my god, that's so romantic," Emory crooned. "Ivy, isn't that romantic?"

Ivy wrapped an arm around Emory's waist. "Sure, babe. Tonight, I'll let you tell me all about Christmas magic while you feed me peppermint stick ice cream."

Emory's eyes glowed. "Awwww, that's so sweet."

"See? I can be romantic," Ivy grumped.

Blake leaned over to whisper something in Trevor's ear and Trevor rolled his eyes. "Just wait for it…" he muttered.

Ivy smirked. "And after that, we'll see about me feeding you a different kind of stick."

Trevor punched Ivy's shoulder while we all laughed at

Ivy's terrible innuendo. Emory was the only one whose eyes bore into his boyfriend, a pretty flush painting his cheeks as he bit his lip.

I had a feeling Emory would be holding Ivy to their little romantic evening later.

We said goodbye and headed toward our getaway location just outside of town beyond the highway.

"This is cute," I said as we unloaded.

The home reminded me of a gingerbread house, not so much in the color scheme—and no candy on the roof—but in the general shape and design. The owners had decorated with precision-perfect big white lights, hanging red icicles, and wreaths donned with huge red bows. The whole look was understated and absolutely gorgeous.

As if reading my mind, Colby whistled as he took in the home.

"Next year, we should hire those guys Emory uses and do the outside of the house. Maybe something like this, or go a bit more over the top? I'm not talking Griswold level, but don't want to look lame next to the Old Christmas House," Colby said, hefting his bag onto his shoulder as he pulled up the entry code on his phone. "Elsie will be old enough to really like the lights next year."

Next year.

My gooey heart sighed.

This was it.

If I had a notebook, I'd be doodling hearts and flowers around our names.

Colby Burke loves Kai Jackson

Kai David and Colby Garrison

Kai loves Colby

CoJack forever

We were doing this. We were a thing.

My brain tried to argue. "No, remember, we had to accept the fact that Colby would always just be our best friend and nothing else could come from it. And we were *fine* with that. We worked really hard to finally believe that."

But my heart jumped up and down screaming. "Nooooo, this is real. It's happening! We love Colby and he loves us!"

I shook my head to clear away the ridiculousness. "Yeah, next year. Definitely."

"You okay?" Colby asked.

I threw an arm around his shoulder and pulled him close, kissing his head. "Yeah, a thousand percent. Just sometimes get caught up in the fact that nothing has changed even though everything has changed."

He studied me and grinned. "Yeah, I get that."

Once inside, we both froze to take in the beauty before us.

The white tree was even more gorgeous in person than the picture we'd seen. It glittered, covered in white and red lights, adorned in red and white peppermints and candy canes, crystal icicles, and tiny bits of red tinsel.

"It really is just like at the Winter Ball," Colby said. "I mean, without the mascot plastered all over it."

We both laughed thinking of the Peppermint Hollow Pines mascot—an adorable pine tree making a mean face —decorating every spare inch of the school.

"That dance was…" Colby let his words fade.

Tossing our bags to the ground in the corner, I stood next to him. "What?"

He shook his head. "We all went in a big group." He

was quiet for a bit. "I was just figuring out I liked you more than friends—scared to death you'd figure it out and get...mad? Upset? I wanted to ask you to dance—it would have been fine. Everyone pretty much accepted you, and they knew we were attached at the hip. Everyone was dancing with everyone else." He shook his head. "What if I'd asked you to dance? The whole trajectory of our lives could have changed."

I snaked an arm around his waist and pressed into his side. "I wanted to dance with you too. I remember purposely dancing with everyone *but* you in hopes no one would see how badly I wanted it to *be* you." Leaning my head against his, I said, "Why did you think I'd be mad or upset?"

Colby was quiet for several beats. "I didn't want to play into stereotypes. Like if I told you I liked you would it make you think I assumed you liked me just because you were bi?" He shrugged. "It made more sense in my head back then."

I kissed his temple. "I get it. I was highly aware of the cliché bi guy falling for his straight best friend and didn't want to be the poster child—but there I was, falling headfirst, and there wasn't a damn thing I could do about it."

"I'm sorry we missed so much time," Colby murmured. "Feels like it was my fault."

"Nope, no more of that from either of us. We were lucky enough to keep each other as best friends while we lived and learned. Maybe we didn't get together in this new way until now, but we've been together—hearts, minds, souls—since we were five. This is just an added bonus." I cupped his face and brushed a kiss over his lips. "And I plan to enjoy every single second of it."

"And if we figure out we're better together without the sex?" Colby scowled.

"Have you been present during the blow jobs of late?" I asked with a cocked brow.

Colby snorted. "Yeah, okay. We're pretty fire in the bedroom too."

"Damn straight."

He frowned. "I guess I'm not, huh?"

"What?"

"Straight. I guess I'm not."

I peppered kisses to his cheeks and eyelids and forehead. "You are whatever feels right to you. There are a million labels—one might work. Or maybe none of them. All that matters is that you know you're loved."

Colby smiled. "Labels really don't matter to me right now. As long as we agree we're spending the rest of our lives together, I'm good."

"Forever."

The kiss was long and slow. The scent of peppermint on the air as the cozy little home wrapped us up in its holiday warmth. When we broke apart, Colby's eyes burned bright.

"Bedroom?"

We did a little exploration of the house on our way to the bedroom. The whole place was movie-set cute, but the bedroom was almost as impressive as the living room. While Christmas trees adorned nearly every room in the house, the one in the living room was the biggest and most festive. But the one in the bedroom was the prettiest.

Could a Christmas tree be romantic?

The lights were soft pinks and purples. The hues of the lights shone lightly on the pastel pink and purple snowflakes, and pink and purple ribbons snaked through the branches with just the right touch of understated pink and purple feathers.

It could have been gaudy and way over the top.

Instead, the tree stood next to the bedroom fireplace, glowing softly as if to spread its love around the room.

"I want to take more time later, after dinner and showers," Colby said as he dropped both our bags onto the loveseat. "Get a fire going," he whispered, wrapping his arms around me and kissing my neck. "Spend the whole night making love with you."

My heart was done. Game over. This man had owned me from day one. Might as well just scoop the heart goo from my chest and hand it to him.

Colby must have felt my shiver because he chuckled. "Good with that?"

I nodded. "So good." Spreading my hands against his lower back, I reveled in his warmth. Gliding up his torso, savoring the broad strength of his back, his shoulders, I buried my face in his neck. "I love you so fucking much."

Colby tipped my head, catching my mouth in a kiss that seared my soul. His hands tangled in my hair, the slick heat of his tongue filling my mouth, his body pressed against mine. "We can skip dinner," he panted when we broke apart.

I shook my head. "No, I want to go out. With you. But we can get off first."

We wore our standard jeans. Colby had on a flannel over a white t-shirt. I'd opted for a soft sweater. We'd already lost our boots at the door, so stripping to our boxer briefs took very little time at all.

Pushing Colby to the monstrous king-sized bed, I shucked my underwear and gestured for him to do the same. Once we were both naked, I crawled on top of him, straddling his waist, rocking my hips over his hard cock.

"Fuck, I wanna watch you ride me," Colby said, eyes flaming hot with desire.

Nearly breaking my neck, I scrambled from the bed, grabbed the lube from my bag, and pumped a small amount into my palm before tossing the bottle in the general vicinity of the bedside table and returning to my previous position.

I smeared my ass crack with lube, coated Colby's cock, and slicked my dick with the leftovers.

"Wait, I wanna..." Colby's protest died when I shushed him.

Shifting over his lower abdomen until his hard length nestled between my ass cheeks, I rolled my hips. The heat of his cock pressed against me combined with Colby's grunt of pleasure almost undid me right there.

When he gripped my hips, fingertips digging into me, my body begged to forget dinner and just let Colby slide his dick into me.

Instead, because I knew Colby wanted to experience bottoming before he fucked me, I fisted my dick while rocking my hips, letting my ass stroke Colby's cock.

"Fuck, Kai, that's good," Colby muttered, his fiery eyes flitting between my face and where I stroked myself.

One thing about a life-long crush finally coming to fruition and getting the man of your dreams in your bed is the need to build up stamina. Colby and I had discovered we got off a lot more quickly with each other than we ever did before—which made sense since our fantasies were coming true. It wasn't a bad thing, just meant we needed to practice.

And practice.

And practice.

Not exactly a hardship.

Speaking of a *hard* ship, the rocket sliding between my ass cheeks had me nearing blast-off.

"Can you come this way?" I asked, the slick heat of his cock pressing against my hole and balls with each stroke.

Colby grunted and thrust his hips, his fingers still a vice grip on my flesh.

We lost ourselves to the moment. The soft glow of the lights on the tree, the scent of peppermint and sweat, and the soft sound of slick skin filled the air.

"Fuck," Colby gritted out. Fingers digging into my hips, he cursed and stilled. "Fuuuck…" His cock throbbed between my ass cheeks, wet heat slicking my skin as his release erupted.

The orgasm hit hard and fast, my load splattering Colby's chest and abs in thick ropes as I rode out my pleasure.

Shifting to bring our chests together, ignoring the mess we'd made of each other, I kissed him. Groaning as Colby's hand fisted in my hair, I worried my heart would explode from the sheer exultation of being in love with Colby and being able to act on it for the first time in forever.

Breaking the kiss, our lips only a breath apart, Colby's blue eyes flashed in the holiday lights. "I love you so damn much," he growled. "With or without this," he punctuated the words with a thrust of his hips, "I love you."

"CoJack forever," I murmured against his lips.

Colby made a strangled noise and crushed our mouths together again.

Maybe, just maybe, he'd been needing this new development in our relationship just as much as me.

"Quick shower and dinner?" I murmured against his neck several moments later when I'd finally emerged from the orgasm haze.

"And then I'm trapping you in this bed and not letting you leave until we head home."

"I'm not sure that's the threat you think it is. And it's not trapping me if I go willingly," I teased.

"As long as we're both on the same page," Colby said, trailing his hand down my back to grip my ass. "Fuck, I love touching you."

I pushed up on my elbows, bringing my hands to cup the sides of his face. The swell of emotion in my chest nearly choked out my words, but I swallowed and pressed my forehead to his. "I love you. Back then, now, forever. I want to enjoy every single second, but I'm also terrified we'll lose this. Lose what we've always had."

Colby shook his head, his eyes shiny and bright. "We can't lose something we've had for a quarter of a century. It's ours, belongs to us. Like we belong to each other."

Breathing him in, I nodded, my eyes closed as I savored our bodies pressed together in the warm bubble of bliss. "You've always owned me, heart and soul."

Colby snorted and slapped my ass. "Maybe that's why both of us sucked at dating other people."

"Valid point."

We fell into a fit of laughter—hands, lips, and tongues exploring all over as we sank into the easiness of just being together.

This was good. *We* were good. We made sense like nothing in my life had ever made sense.

Several kisses later, I blew a raspberry on his cheek, and we rolled ourselves out of bed, laughing and wrestling all the way to the bathroom.

Twenty minutes later, we'd taken a quick shower and dressed for dinner. Walking hand-in-hand to Colby's truck, I allowed myself to imagine our future.

Like this.

Together.

CoJack forever.

Dinner turned out to be a situation I didn't know I needed. Colby and I had eaten about a million meals together. But we'd never allowed ourselves to let it feel like a date.

Never held hands.

Never asked for a corner booth in the back.

And never sat pressed so close together in the curved booth as we studied the menu.

Once the waitperson had taken our orders, Colby pulled out his phone. "I can't wait any longer," he said with a sheepish shrug.

When I gave him a questioning look, he tapped the video button to call my mom's phone.

I sighed. "Oh, thank god. I didn't know how to interrupt our date, but I'm dying to see her."

Mom answered and immediately moved to the living room where my dad and Elsie were playing on the floor. Elsie squealed, blew raspberries, and reached for the phone while Colby and I made complete fools of ourselves talking to her in our daddy voices.

She lost interest fairly quickly when my dad sat her up between his legs and she started grabbing for a soft rattle he handed to her.

Mom assured us Elsie was doing great and everything had gone smoothly so far. "Your dad and I, and Tom and Allison, decided to get a bed for the guest room and a bed for Elsie's room. We'll send you the pictures and you can tell us if you hate the styles, but they can be delivered tomorrow. Dad and Tom can get everything set up. When you boys get home, Elsie can start taking naps in her own room."

"Mom, you didn't have to do that," I started.

"We were going to get things set up soon," Colby added.

"We all wanted to help," Mom said. "Consider it Christmas."

"You already got us gifts; I've seen them under your tree."

Mom waved away the protest. "Then a celebration gift for you two finally getting together."

Knowing there was no use arguing, I told my mom thank you, let Colby do the same, and then made sure they were set for overnight with the baby.

About two minutes after we disconnected the video, my phone buzzed with a text from my mom. There were about ten pictures of a queen-sized bed and a baby bed with a message stating, "If you don't like these, go to this link, and pick out what you prefer. I want to order before bed so they can get it here tomorrow."

Our drinks arrived along with a basket of rolls as we studied the two beds.

"Do you like them?" I asked.

Colby gave a disgruntled look but nodded. "I wanted to hate them so we can tell them no, but they're great."

I took his hand. "We don't have to get them. I'll tell her we want to do it ourselves if you'd rather."

He shook his head. "No, it's really nice of them. I think I'm just not in love with the idea of Elsie having her own room. Which is dumb because I know she needs to have her own space."

"Baby steps," I assured him, my thumb rubbing over his knuckles. "We don't even have to start with her taking naps in there." Leaning in, I breathed deeply of his soap, cologne, and the natural scent of Colby. "Plus, there's a bed in the guest room now. Nap times just got a lot more comfortable for our...um...activities."

Colby shivered and pressed into me. "Good point. We can take things as they feel right."

I texted my mom to let her know we were good with her selections and put my phone to the side. When a large group of diners filed past our table, I instinctively let go of Colby's hand on the off chance we'd know someone—we were barely outside of Peppermint Hollow. "Sorry," I muttered.

Colby shot a glance toward the group and back at me before grabbing my hand and lacing our fingers together. "Don't be sorry about shit, Kai. I'm not ashamed of you or us. If we're doing this—and I'll be damned if anyone tries to tell us we aren't doing this—we're doing it right. I'm all in."

I gave his fingers a squeeze. "Just didn't know where

you were with being in a relationship with a guy. Didn't want to out you if you weren't ready."

Colby leaned in and kissed me. "I think it would take a little getting used to if I were trying to date just any guy, but not with you. We've been attached at the hip since we were five. People have always thought we were a thing anyway." He frowned. "Oh shit, I'm sorry. Would you rather not be open about being in a relationship with a guy? Or with me?"

Unlacing our fingers, I studied his face, keeping my features neutral.

Then I dropped a hand to his thigh and squeezed hard enough to make Colby grunt. "What the fuck, man?" he asked with a chuckle as he rubbed his leg.

I gripped his chin and brought his face to mine, nose-to-nose. "Don't be a dumbass. I've wanted to be able to hold your hand, kiss you, and call you my boyfriend in public since I was sixteen."

"Okay, okay," Colby said, bringing a hand to my side for a soft caress.

Just as I melted into the moment, he jabbed his fingers into my ribs.

Before we could break into full-on wrestling in the booth, our server arrived with a tray of food.

We straightened up in our seats, both looking like children who got caught doing something wrong. Colby cleared his throat. I covered a cough.

Our server smirked and placed our food on the table.

We lingered over a light meal, savored our wine, and eventually ordered dessert to go. Holding hands as we made our way to the parking lot, I knew our first date of the rest of our lives would always hold a special place in my heart.

Back at the cozy little rental, I opted for the hall bathroom and told Colby to take his time in the big bathroom off our bedroom. I'd packed us both prep supplies, and I knew Colby had practiced prepping a few times, but I wanted him to have as stress-free a first time as possible.

Passing him on the way to the hall, I pulled him into a kiss. "You can change your mind at any time. None of what we are hinges on sex. Top or bottom, now or never, nothing changes what I feel for you." Brushing the pads of my thumbs over his cheeks, I pressed our foreheads together and just appreciated the warm scent of Colby in my arms. "You got me?"

He nodded. "I know. I'm not nervous—" He broke off with a nervous laugh. "Okay, I'm nervous, but it's more excited anticipation than bad nerves. I want this with you so damn bad. Been wanting it for years if I'm honest. It's almost... it's like being with you like this is the missing part of what we've had for so long."

I shook my head. "Sex doesn't solve everything," I started.

"I know." He shut me up with a kiss. "I'm not looking for this to solve anything. But there's been an empty space in my heart since...forever. The only time I've ever felt close to being whole is when I'm with you." He kissed me again. "Taking this step may not fill that space, but there's no one I'd rather share this with than you." Colby rubbed his nose against mine. "You got me?"

Grinning, I nodded. "I got you. Now, go get ready 'cause we've got plans."

Colby cocked a brow.

Gesturing toward the bed, I nodded. "Bed, lube, you, me..."

Colby groaned and we lost ourselves in another long, slow kiss.

We finally separated for our showers, both of us taking time to ready our bodies for a level of connection we'd never shared with each other.

When I walked into the bedroom, a fire burned bright and warm in the fireplace. The bed was turned down. And the scent of shampoo, body wash, and peppermint hung on the air.

Colby stood in the middle of the room in nothing but boxer briefs. As I closed the door behind me, he tapped something on his phone and placed it on the bedside table.

A song from long ago filled the air.

And I knew this man was my forever.

CHAPTER 14

COLBY

Kai's eyes flew to mine as the first notes of "I Won't Give Up" by Jason Mraz filled the air. He flung his towel to the side, never taking his eyes from me.

I knew he recognized the song and why I'd chosen it. The DJ had played it twice during the Winter Ball in January of our senior year. The year I'd finally admitted I felt something more than friendship for my best friend. I'd wanted to dance with Kai so damn bad, but I'd been confused as hell. Things with my mom were absolute shit at all times, but that day had been particularly bad. Add that to the epiphany I'd had about wanting to kiss Kai, and I was a hot mess with zero clue what to do about anything. Give in and possibly fuck things up beyond recognition? Or play it cool, bottling things up and burying them deep, and keep my best friend by my side?

Holding out my hand, I willed my heart not to beat out of my chest and thanked the universe for giving me the chance for a do-over. "Dance with me?"

A smile softened Kai's gorgeous face as he took my

hand. "This was playing at the Winter Ball. Twice, I think."

Clearing my throat, I nodded. "I might have made a playlist of the songs from that night. Listened to it for years."

In just our boxers, we swayed slowly, arms snaked around each other, bodies pressed together, hearts thumping in twin rhythms.

"I played this song about a million times; always thought of it as our song," Kai said, pressing the side of his face to mine. "In the beginning, all I focused on was the *I won't give up* part of the lyrics. Then I convinced myself it was the part about in the end we're still friends." He shook his head, breathing deeply.

With my entire body on fire, wanting to crawl under his skin, I held Kai tight as we rocked together to the music, listening as he rambled. "And now?"

"I realize this song is so damn perfect for us—some ways the same, some ways different." The memories of our friendship washed over us. "The part about needing space to navigate—I think it applies to both of us. We both needed that time." Kai's words caught in his throat. "And this part…"

The song filled the air, cloaking us in memories and promises as the artist belted out a line about learning who he was and who he wasn't.

I took a shaky breath. "Yeah, back then, I had no clue who I was—or, I thought I knew who I was and it wasn't worth loving. I would have been a disaster if we'd gotten together."

"And I needed time to figure my own shit out. I always knew I'd take our friendship over anything else, but I had to come to terms with a lot of my emotions over you."

The song started again and we grinned at each other, melting into the moment, a perfect mixture of the past and the present.

We swayed, singing the song with our foreheads resting together.

As the song neared the end, I stole a kiss. "We *do* have a lot to learn," I said, referring to the lyrics. "At least this part of we does."

Kai nodded. "We both do. But we're tough and we're worth it, even when things get rough."

"I'm not giving up," I whispered.

"Me neither. Forever."

My playlist went on to play other songs from our senior year Winter Ball and my heart took flight. Looking forward to years of dancing with my best friend as we journeyed through our life—*together* together—wasn't something I'd dreamed of forever, but it was the very dream I hadn't known I'd been desperate for.

Between the nearly naked dancing and the sweet, whispered words, our bodies grew impatient with the vertical contact. I caressed my hands up and down Kai's back, loving the broad strength of him in my arms. "I want you," I murmured against his lips.

Kai gripped the back of my head, fingers tight in my hair, and sucked on my bottom lip as he pushed toward the bed. "Take 'em off," he said as he shucked his underwear. Giving me a great view of his ass, he searched the floor, and produced the bottle of lube I'd tossed carelessly earlier. Placing it on the bedside table, Kai stood next to the bed, stroking himself as he watched me.

Rolling to my side, I reached out to grab him by the ass and pulled him closer. Swallowing his dick, welcoming his unique flavor, I swirled my tongue. I could have sucked him all night. The weight of his cock on my tongue was a drug I couldn't get enough of.

Kai groaned and pushed at my shoulder, rolling me to my stomach. "Lift your ass," he demanded. And fuck, why did bossy Kai send heat straight to my balls? "You still want to take me?"

"Fuck, yes," I mumbled into the sheet, lifting on slightly bent knees. I wasn't sure I'd want to bottom all the time, but I was dead set on knowing what it felt like to take a cock before I fucked Kai. Sure, I could play around with a toy, but I had a very interested dick attached to a very hot and willing guy at my disposal. Why not take the real thing if it was available and offered?

He positioned himself between my spread legs, shoulders pressed against the back of my thighs, and buried his face in my ass. The strangled cry escaping me barely had time to fill the air before Kai's tongue swiped over my hole.

Kai had introduced me to the joys of rimming early on in our physical relationship, and I wasn't the least bit upset about it. Something I'd never done with others had quickly become one of my favorite things to do with Kai. Maybe because it was an act I shared with only him.

Or maybe—

"Fucking hell," I moaned into the mattress as Kai's tongue teased my hole, working me open, getting me sloppy wet.

As I was saying, maybe it was because it was Kai.

Maybe it was because having his tongue pressed into me was fucking heavenly.

Either way, I was a fan.

Kai reached for my dick, stroking me as he ate my ass. When he shifted his position and tapped a spit-slick finger at my hole, I shivered with anticipation.

"This okay?" Kai asked.

"Fuck, yes. But I don't wanna come this way."

He finger-fucked me while fondling my balls and running his thumb over my leaking slit. Just when I was about to give in and beg him to make me come—we had all night, I could bottom for him later—Kai pulled his fingers from my body and pressed a kiss to my hole.

"Get on top," Kai ordered.

With my sex-crazed head doing its best to keep up, I turned to look at him as he positioned himself on his back. "I wanna feel you on top of me." Fuck. The image of Kai between my spread legs, thrusting his cock into my ass, making love to me…well, it was definitely a scene I'd jerked off to more than once.

"You will. But the first time you take me it's best if you're on top. Just for a bit. You can control things better that way." He gripped his cock and licked his lips, waggling his brows in the most ridiculously salacious way. "Climb on."

This.

I needed Kai like this.

The perfect combination of mind-blowing sex while still being my ridiculous best friend. I'd never laughed with anyone during sex. Never looked at someone and thought about how lucky I was to have them in my life.

Never wanted to just roll into their arms and let them hold me all night.

Until Kai.

He was different.

We were different.

CoJack forever.

Grabbing the lube first, I moved to straddle Kai's waist.

"Let me do that," Kai said, taking the lube from my hand. He pumped the bottle a few times and reached to slick his cock and my ass. Working the lube into my tight pucker, Kai let his other hand caress up and down my chest and torso, teasing my nipples.

He tossed the lube to the side and gripped my thighs.

"It's your show," he said.

Kai's cockhead pressed against my tight ring and I lowered myself a fraction, hands braced on his chest, his touch light on my skin.

Waiting.

I was wet and open from his tongue and fingers, but nothing had prepared me, not really. The stinging flash of heated pain took my breath and froze me in place.

Kai ran a gentle hand up my thigh and over my ass. With his other, he took my hand and brought it to his mouth. Soft kisses against my palm promising patience and forever. "Do you need to stop?"

Shaking my head, I took a deep breath and shifted down, another inch of Kai's slick dick sliding into me.

And then another.

And another.

Until my balls pressed against his lower abs and my ass rested atop his thighs.

My body was a mixed bag of grumbled protests against the intrusion and murmured pleas to keep him inside me forever.

"You good?" Kai asked.

I nodded and rolled my hips, gasping at the zing of pleasure.

Kai's hands returned to grip my thighs, my ass, anywhere he could get a good hold. Strong fingers pressed into my skin. Big hands held me. But the moment was also thumbs stroking gently over hip bones, fingers feathering appreciatively over our connection.

"Fuck, Colby." Kai's strangled words pushed through my sex-fogged brain.

Shifting slightly, I brought my chest to his, our faces millimeters apart. "Kai…"

It was a curse, a prayer, a promise.

A plea.

Pressing our foreheads together, Kai hitched a breath and nodded. His eyes closed, one hand gripping my neck, one on the small of my back. He held me there.

Held me as his cock throbbed inside me.

Held me as our hearts beat as one.

Held me as our friendship transcended everything we'd been before.

But even then, nothing really changed. Kai was still the boy whose smile had lit me on fire since I was eighteen. The boy who protected my heart from the shit of my past. Who loved me just as I was through bad decisions and worse decisions.

Kai.

My best friend.

My heart and soul.

My forever.

He took a shaky breath and gently rocked his hips. "I love you," he whispered against my lips.

"Thank you for waiting," I said. "For not giving up on my stupid ass."

Kai grinned. Even in the dimly lit room, his eyes sparkled. "I would never give up on you, even if it meant giving up on us."

"There is no me without us."

"Fuck, Cole."

He rolled me to my back, gently pushing my legs apart. Applying more lube to my ass and his cock first, Kai pressed kisses to both knees. Guiding his cock to my hole, Kai brought his chest down to mine and caught my mouth in a searing kiss as he breached my tight muscle again. He captured my gasp of pleasure just as he pulled out and slowly slid back in.

We were as connected as two people could be, but my body longed for more—to meld into him, to crawl under his skin, and never break apart. With arms wrapped around his torso, I held onto Kai as he pumped in and out of me.

Making love wasn't something I'd ever done.

Until now.

Until Kai.

He poured himself into me. Every drop of love and lust over the last decade painted each movement, each heavy breath, each slick slide into my body.

And never once did he look away. Never lost himself to only the physical act. Kai's eyes held mine. His big hands cupping my face, our noses brushing as he made love to me.

I'd wanted to flip with him, take turns fucking each other, but now all I wanted was to shatter with him. To come apart around him while he filled me with his release. "Fuck, Kai." My words ragged with emotion. "Fuck, wanna come with you."

Fire lit Kai's eyes and he made quick work of maneuvering a pillow under my ass before he increased the speed and strength of his thrusts. With his arms anchored under my shoulders and the new angle of my hips, Kai's cockhead brushed over my prostate with each and every thrust. My world whited out, the electric pleasure heating me from the inside out.

"Colby. Fuck." Kai's breathing was fast and heavy. "I'm close."

Our bodies pressed together, my leaking cock trapped between us, the hot friction close to sending me into orbit. "Do it," I begged. "Come in me, wanna feel it."

Kai threaded his fingers into the hair at the back of my head and gripped tightly. "Tell me why."

He knew my fantasy. And I knew it turned him on as much as it did me.

"Wanna feel you unload in me. Be the only person to fill me with your cum."

Kai thrust harder, his eyes never leaving mine.

"Then later, when I'm fucking you," I went on, panting and whimpering with each pump of his hips, "I wanna feel your cum dripping from my ass as I'm coming inside you. The very last person to ever paint your pretty hole with cum."

"Holy shit." Kai's voice faltered along with his rhythm. He dropped his head to my neck and groaned, his hips freezing as his dick pumped his release.

Kai's wrecked words and his pulsating cock were too much. The orgasm rolled over me, sweet and hot, spilling between us.

"Fucking hell," Kai murmured a few moments later.

"That good? Or that bad?" I asked. Mostly teasing, but suddenly overcome with doubt.

Kai grabbed my face and kissed me. His tongue aggressively sweet. "Even if this wasn't forever, you just fucking ruined me for anyone else."

"Really?"

Kai feathered kisses over my eyelids. "Never been that good."

Pride punched my heart.

"You're okay? It was good for you?" Kai asked, concern etching his face. "I've never been someone's first."

"First and last," I reminded him, unsure of where the prick of tears had come from.

When we finally broke apart, Kai grabbed his discarded towel and cleaned us up. We opted to sleep first, shower later, and cuddled together in a bed we'd most definitely be changing the sheets on before we ended our stay.

CHAPTER 15

KAI

SLEEP CAME EASILY AFTER MIND-BLOWING orgasms, but the intense newness of what Colby and I had woke us not long into our slumber. Hands and mouths exploring quickly turned to me on my back, legs spread, gasping as Colby kissed my neck and sucked my nipples.

He rocked his hips, our hard cocks sliding together. "Fuck, I could come just like this," he said. "Just lookin' at you."

"Or you could get that dick in me," I said, gripping his ass and pulling as if I could absorb him into my skin.

"Greedy," Colby said, but he reached for the lube.

"Yep." I stroked my cock. "Been waiting for this for too long."

Colby smeared lube into my hole, stretching me open.

Knowing I should have let him work me open a bit longer, but unable to fight back the urge to have him inside me, I reached for him. Stilling his arm, I met his eyes. "Please." Only one word, but he knew what I wanted.

Slicking his cock with the leftover lube and adding a bit more, Colby slotted himself between my legs. The look of awe and love, eyes filled with gentle heat, took my breath away.

I'd been waiting for this.

Waiting for him.

Waiting for something I'd accepted would never happen.

As he slid into me, his thick heat invading my body, pushing through the tight ring of muscle, I knew what it meant to have a dream come true.

The deeper meaning of souls melding into one.

We were more than sex, of that, I had no doubt.

But taking him into my body, connecting with Colby in the only way we'd never shared, sent goosebumps over my skin, and had my chest so warm and full of love I struggled to take a proper breath.

"This okay?" Colby asked, voice taut as he held himself still.

"God, yes," I whined.

He let out a breath and surged deeper, making me cry out. Then he set a slow, easy rhythm of in and out that lit me on fire.

But I wanted more.

"Colby. Fuck," I gritted out.

"What do you want?" he asked, his big hand caressing my face, moving to grab a pec, teasing over the nipple, and squeezing.

"Over the bed. Fuck me," I begged.

Colby cursed, leaning in to kiss me. Our tongues slick and hot as he rocked into me over and over. "Bend over," he said, slipping from my body and moving back to give me room.

Bent over the bed, my legs spread for him wasn't a position I'd ever taken for other lovers. I was open, vulnerable, and so damn turned on I almost nutted against the mattress.

"Shit," I mumbled, gripping my dick as I reached for a towel to protect the bed that wasn't ours.

Colby took his place between my legs, nestling his hot, hard length between my ass cheeks as he leaned over me. With his chest pressed to my back and lips feathering kisses to my neck, he whispered, "You are so fucking gorgeous."

Bucking my hips, a keening noise escaping me, I gripped the sheets. "Fuck, Colby, please. Give it to me." I'd never begged a man to fuck me. Never felt that searing need all the way to my core. But everything with Colby was new and right, and I longed for him to fill me up.

Colby straightened and pressed his cock against my hole. With twin groans filling the air around us, he slid into me as my body opened, welcoming him home.

Big hands gripped my hips, fingers digging into my flesh as Colby pumped his cock into me over and over. The slick heat, the sweet sting, and the fullness all spelled out how complete and right we were together.

"Fuck, Kai. You look so good on my cock," Colby gritted out, never slowing his thrusts. "Fuck. Wish you could see how pretty you are spread open and taking me so good."

Holy.

Fucking.

Shit.

My best friend was a smooth-ass dirty talker.

Who knew?

And I was one hundred percent here for it.

"Yeah?" I grunted. "Tell me."

Colby bent over me, bringing his mouth to my ear. "Fucking hell, Kai. I could watch my cock fuck into your pretty hole all damn day. The way you open for me, your skin clinging to me as I pull out, stretching around me when I push back in. Wanna fill you with my cum."

His words sent shivers through me, and I whimpered. "Do it. Fuck, Colby, fill me up."

Colby ran both hands from my shoulders, to my elbows, to my wrists. Gently pulling my arms straight, he threaded our fingers together, his pumping hips never faltering. Bringing our arms under my chest, Colby held me tight, his body curved protectively around me.

The friction of my dick against the bed, Colby's cock punching my prostate with each thrust, and the deliciously dirty words he whispered in my ear had me mere seconds from detonation.

"Colby, fuck me. Go hard. Come in me," I begged.

He grunted, breathing heavily as he increased the speed and power of his thrusts. "Fuck," he bit out. "Fuck, Kai." He buried his face in my neck. "Fucking hell, baby. I can feel it. Feel your cum leaking from my ass."

That was all it took for both of us to explode.

I turned my head and let Colby devour my mouth as my throbbing cock spilled over the towel. Colby's dick pulsed in my ass, the wet heat of his cum adding to the slick slide of flesh against flesh.

He collapsed onto my back, breaths heavy and fast, warm kisses to my shoulders and neck. "Fuck."

I chuckled. "Yeah. That was…"

Colby froze. "Was it bad?"

"Fucking hell, man. That was the best I've ever had."

Colby's chest expanded against my back and I heard the smile in his words. "Yeah, it really was."

I squeezed his hands still tucked under my chest. "I love you."

"Because I'm a sex god?" Colby teased, his breath hot against my ear.

"Takes one to know one," I shot back.

Our laughter turned to pathetic moans when Colby slipped from my ass.

"I love you too," he said. "But now, I need sleep." He yawned and stood up straight before making his way to the bathroom for another towel.

Once cleaned up, ignoring the fact we desperately needed to shower—exhaustion won out—we curled together in the dimly lit room and slept.

I woke several hours later, if the sunlight streaming into the room was any indication, with Colby's rock-hard cock pressed against my ass. His hand traveled down my arm to my hip bone before gripping my morning erection. "Good morning," he growled at my ear.

"Good morning," I said on a sigh, loving the warm strength of his hand stroking me.

"How sore are you?" he asked, rocking his hips against me.

"Not too bad," I answered. "Got something in mind?"

Colby rolled his hips. "Can you take me again?"

"Fuck." I whimpered. "Yes."

Colby ran a thumb over my leaking slit before gripping my knee and pressing it to the bed. With my ass spread open for him, Colby guided his cock to my hole and pushed through the ring of muscle. The invasion pulled a cry from me, the sweet sting of exquisite pleasure washing over me as he slid home.

"Fuck, Kai, you're still slick with my cum," he murmured at my ear.

I shivered thinking of his cock sliding into my hole still slick with lube and cum from earlier. "Give me more, make me yours."

Colby threw his arm around my chest and yanked me tightly against him. "No one else will ever fuckin' touch you," he growled. "Mine." He thrust harder.

A breath shuddered from me as love and desire, lightning-hot, shot through me. "Yours. Fuck, Colby. Always yours."

It wasn't just the sex talking. We'd belonged to each other for a quarter of a century, we'd just finally wised up and could talk about it now.

"You own me," Colby whispered, slowing his thrusts. "CoJack forever." His cock slid in and out of my messy hole, the sound of sex filling the air. "Touch yourself."

Taking my throbbing cock in hand, I moaned. Jerking myself to the rhythm of Colby's thrusts, I was soon a babbling, begging mess. Pleading for Colby to make me come and give me his load.

When his hips froze and liquid heat filled me as Colby grunted out his release, I gave into the orgasm and spilled all over my fist.

The rest of our weekend was spent much the same as the first half. Between calls home to check on Elsie, we feasted on carry-out, binged movies, and took uninterrupted naps when we weren't having the best sex of our lives.

Eventually, though, we had to admit we'd nearly sexed ourselves out and needed a break. We finally broke out the Welcome folder the owners had left for guests and discovered a jacuzzi and sauna out back. We vegged out in both several times, making out, laughing, talking about Elsie, and looking forward to the future.

"Do you want to go do something since we're on our own?" I asked Colby.

He'd shaken his head, not even opening his eyes from his relaxed position in the hot tub. "No. We can't have much of this at home. We can take Elsie pretty much anywhere we'd want to go, she's easy like that. She's *not* easy when it comes to giving us time to rest. So, I say we enjoy this and we can plan trips with her and the guys."

Which sounded absolutely perfect to me.

When our weekend away came to an end, we were sure to tidy up and wash the sheets. We left the bed unmade with the clean sheets folded neatly at the foot, but there was no way we were leaving a pile of cum-covered sheets for the owners to wash.

We rushed home, ignoring our parents' assurances that everything was fine and to take as long as we wanted. We needed to get ready for the week at work, but more than anything, we'd missed our baby terribly.

About a week before Christmas, the three of us spent the day at Ivy and Emory's place. Emory had planned a mimosa brunch followed by coffee and chocolate, peppermint-stick ice cream sundaes. We all got to taste the lovely chicory-flavored coffee from the special mugs, but Colby and I opted for regular with cream and sugar.

"Stop telling them it's from the lead-based paint," Emory groused at Ivy, but love and affection shone brightly in his eyes.

The six of us had opened gifts from each other, and Colby and I protested about how much the guys had spoiled Elsie with over-the-top gifts. An indoor slide she wouldn't be able to use for a while, a water and sand table for the patio, and a coupon for babysitting from the four of them.

"That's only good for a dinner date, no overnights," Ivy grumbled.

"And all four of us have to be available," Trevor added, fear glowing in his eyes.

"Don't listen to them, they're chickens." Emory picked Elsie up and tickled her belly, making her laugh. "I'll babysit any time you need me."

Magic let out a quiet woof.

"Me and Magic," Emory amended.

As the day drew to a close and the sun sank below the horizon, casting Peppermint Hollow into wintery dusk, we said our goodbyes, bundled Elsie up, and headed across the side street toward home.

Colby grabbed my elbow as we reached the front sidewalk. A man stood on our front steps.

Jerking me toward the pine tree in the front yard, Colby motioned for me to stay there with Elsie. From our hiding spot, we watched. The man peered into the window, cupping his hand to his eyes. Stepping back, he took an envelope from his inside coat pocket and dropped in into our mailbox.

Then he walked toward a dark sedan parked across the street, gave the house a once-over, and climbed into his car. Taillights vanished down the street.

"What the fuck was that?" I asked.

Colby bristled beside me. "I don't know, but I don't like it."

A chilly wind swirled around us just as icy fingers dug into my heart.

CHAPTER 16

COLBY

No matter how many times I read the letter, it never got better. My insides churned; terror infected my every heartbeat, seeping into each breath as I attempted to navigate the fear.

Kai and I hadn't slept a wink, so the morning found us running on copious amounts of caffeine. Jitters and dread meshed with exhaustion were the worst combination.

We'd called in the troops as soon as the sun was up enough to be considered an appropriate time to text. No one was dying—despite my entire existence being awash in soul-clenching trepidation—and there was no reason to wake others up before dawn just because we hadn't slept.

The entire crew—our parents and the guys—arrived with coffee, breakfast, and fearful curiosity. Having them there didn't solve anything—at least not yet—but my heart at least slowed to under Mach 10 with the reinforcements.

Kai and I had spent our sleepless night huddled

together between taking care of Elsie's bottles and diapers. We imagined the worst, voiced fear and anger, pondered potential solutions, and held each other in brain-and-heart-weary stupors.

Upon walking through the door, Lacy immediately picked Elsie up, sitting down on the couch next to Kai with our daughter in her arms. Allison took a seat on the floor, leaning up next to the arm of the couch right next to me.

My dad, Ivy, Trevor, and Blake stood with arms crossed as if ready to defend us until the end.

Emory and Kai's dad took one look at us and then the letter on the coffee table. Eric grabbed the piece of paper and glanced over it. "Copier?" he asked.

Emory pulled on Eric's elbow, and they disappeared to where we kept our little office copier. Five minutes later, they were back, distributing copies of the letter to everyone.

Horror and anger simmered as our friends and family read the words we'd read a million times.

"Is this even legal?"

"Can they do this?"

"No, I thought you said she signed those papers."

"I have a good attorney."

"Oh my god, no, they can't do this."

"We'll fight it. No way they're getting away with this."

My dad gritted his teeth, grip tight on the letter. "What do you know? I assume you've looked into this guy?"

I rubbed my eyes. "Frederick Earnst has a flashy webpage with a bunch of testimonials. He specializes in custodial cases but has also done a lot with accident and injury cases. He has a *Contact Me Now* button where website visitors can give him all the details and he'll reach out to them to let them know if he thinks he can win the case. Everything on his site makes him look successful, hard-nosed, and he promises he doesn't get paid unless he wins your case."

"But?" Trevor asked.

"Looking into him away from his website, he's got tons of complaints. He's been reported to the Better Business Bureau multiple times."

"So, basically a slimy ambulance chaser, but with custody cases." Blake grimaced.

I nodded. "Yeah."

"We already contacted our attorney," Kai said, his hand squeezing mine. He'd been my rock since the letter had been delivered, even though I knew he was just as terrified as me. "He put us in touch with the family law attorney who looked over Sasha's termination of parental rights paperwork. Name's Jaxon Wright. We have a call with him this morning."

Jaxon had told us not to reply to the letter from Frederick Earnst. Said he'd never had dealings with the man, but he'd known other scumbags just like him. We were to discuss things with Mr. Wright only and let him do the work for us. He stated again that Sasha's parental rights termination papers had been valid and would hold up in court.

Hopefully, what Frederick Earnst was coming at us with would turn out to be bullshit. But the threat was very real, eating away at my soul. The words of the letter mocked me from the page, making me doubt everything I thought I knew.

Mr. Colby Burke,
RE: NOTICE OF POTENTIAL CUSTODY ACTION

We hope this letter finds you well. My name is Frederick Earnst of Earnst & Co. Attorney at Law, and I am the attorney representing the noncustodial grandparents, Carl and Lea Klein, in their pursuit of custody of Elsie Mae Burke.

After recently discovering the existence of their only grandchild, the grandparents have decided to seek custody. First and foremost, please understand that our intention is not to disrupt the familial relationships or cause any undue stress. Our primary concern is the well-being and best interests of Elsie. It is in this spirit that we have taken on this responsibility.

We understand that this may be a difficult and sensitive situation for you, and we are open to exploring amicable solutions that prioritize the child's well-being. Our goal is to reach a resolution that serves the best interests of [insert child's name here] while also maintaining a harmonious family dynamic.

We encourage you to reach out to us at your earliest convenience to discuss this matter further. We are available to address any concerns or questions you may have and to explore potential avenues for resolution.

Thank you for your attention to this matter. We look forward to a constructive dialogue and a resolution that prioritizes the best interests of the child.

It was a damn form letter. Whoever wrote it hadn't even properly filled in all the blanks. This man sent this letter out enough times to need a fucking template. Nothing about it was in the best interest of my child. How many lives had he ruined with this letter?

And Sasha's parents.

Fuck. Them.

The crew settled into circle-the-wagons mode. Ivy came and went between appointments at the shop. Allison left for a bit to meet with two clients at the salon. Dad and Eric checked in on us but spent most of the time in the garage.

Trevor and Blake left for a bit to get some work done but promised to return later with dinner for everyone.

Emory and Lacy took over with Elsie and hovered over Kai and me like mother hens.

The call with Jaxon Wright went well.

He answered our questions and shared his thoughts as well as next steps.

"Mainly, the letter is a scare tactic. It's full of reassurances to get you thinking it can be handled amicably, but if you were to reach out to Earnst I guarantee he'd strike like a pit viper," Wright explained. "You've got a solid foundation to stand on with the mother's termination of custodial rights—if she hadn't provided that, we may be looking at a messier situation—and the noncustodial grandparents have very little to stand on as long as the child isn't deemed to be in an unsafe situation."

"Could they say she's in harm's way due to us being a same-sex partnership?" Kai asked.

I knew immediately where his head was. He'd leave us. Kai would let go of what we had if it meant making it easier for me to keep Elsie.

I gripped his hand, swallowing down the urge to vomit, and shook my head at him.

He gave me a sad smile and shrugged.

"They might try, but it would only stand up if they could prove Elsie's physical, emotional, and psychological development were being threatened." Wright sighed. "I guess we could get really unlucky and get a homophobic judge, but that's a bridge we'll cross if and when we get to it."

Wright wrapped up the call with his next steps and that he'd be in touch.

"Maybe you and Elsie should go live with your parents?" Kai asked, his words barely a whisper, his skin tinged with green.

I gripped his chin. "I will do anything for my daughter, but we will fight this together. You hear me?"

"CoJack forever," Kai murmured, tears sparkling in his eyes.

"Damn straight." I pressed a firm kiss to his forehead.

"Then we fight with everything we have."

Emory bustled into the room with drinks and snacks for us before getting down on the floor with Magic and Elsie to play.

Lacy joined them and soon Elsie's infectious laughter filled the room, easing the pain and panic in my heart just a bit.

Emory was telling Lacy about the mistletoe that mysteriously appeared in their home during the holiday season.

"Like the stockings that showed up here?" Kai's mom asked.

Kai sighed as every eye ventured toward the perfect-match stockings on the mantle. "I'm not sure we've got the Christmas magic here, Mom. If we did, we sure could use it right about now."

Emory shoved his glasses up his nose and glanced toward the three round ornaments on the tree. Two teal and one silver. Kai, me, and Elsie. "I don't know, but if ever there's a time for that special, sometimes unexplained vibe of the holidays to kick in and help things work out, now is definitely the time."

Maybe it was my exhausted mind playing tricks, or maybe just a reflection, but I swore the three ornaments gleamed brighter in the glow of the twinkling lights.

※

Our life stopped in the days leading up to Christmas.

Kai and I somehow got the essentials with work done each day.

Our parents and friends stayed close by.

And we sat on pins and needles for updates from Jaxon.

He'd reached out to Frederick Earnst but was only able to leave a message. The answering service indicated he was out of the office for the holidays.

The day before Christmas Eve—Kai and I were in no mood to celebrate, but we kept it together for Elsie's sake —Jaxon called us.

"Well, I finally got in touch with Earnst. He called today."

"And?" I was going to barf.

"He stated he was no longer representing the Kleins and hung up on me."

Silence while his words registered.

"That's good, right?" Kai asked.

Wright sighed. "I'd like to think so, but it could just mean the Kleins figured out he was a sleazeball and took their business to someone more reputable."

"So, it's not over." The tiny crystal of hope I'd allowed to form in my gut shattered into a million shards.

"Can't really say," Jaxon said. "I don't think much will happen over the holidays. I'll keep in touch, but I think your best bet is to try to put this behind you and enjoy your time with family. We can face it head-on, if needed, in the new year."

Like a person with only days left to live being told there had been a mistake and they'd live a long, happy life, Kai and I moved through the rest of the day in a stupor. Confusion, doubt, hope, and relief melted together and kept us from taking deep breaths.

Our families and friends went home, buoyed by what they were taking as good news, leaving us to weather the storm of *what now*, waiting for the other shoe to drop.

We ate an early dinner.

Gave Elsie her bath.

And attempted to get ourselves into the holiday spirit.

Then, while Elsie played, bouncing and squealing in her activity center, a knock sounded at the door.

Kai and I stood.

He took my hand. "CoJack forever."

I gave a nod and moved toward the door as Kai picked up Elsie and held her close.

On the other side of the door stood two strangers I'd never seen before.

But the man had his daughter's eyes.

The woman had her smile.

Sasha's parents.

CHAPTER 17

KAI

I KNEW BY COLBY'S DEFENSIVE STANCE AND quick intake of breath that the couple at the door were Elsie's grandparents.

Sasha's mom and dad.

The man cleared his throat. "I'm Carl Klein. This is my wife, Lea. We're so sorry to barge in, but I think we've made a terrible mistake."

"Please," Lea interrupted. "Please let us fix what we've done."

I kept Elsie snug in my arms as she peeked at the strangers.

Colby stepped back to allow them entrance.

I didn't want them in our house, but I gritted my teeth and motioned them toward the living room.

"I apologize for sounding rude...no, fuck that, I don't care if I sound rude. Why are you here?" Colby bit out.

"We are so very sorry," Lea said. "We were elated when Sasha reached out to us; we hadn't heard from her in two years. She said she wanted to see us." Lea's face clouded.

"The visit didn't go well," Carl interjected.

"They never do," Lea said.

Colby grunted.

"She was high when we got to the restaurant. Told us she only had time for lunch because she was leaving soon, flying back to a man in France." Carl glanced toward Elsie, a slight smile on his face.

"Sasha isn't an easy person even when she's not under the influence," Lea said. "When she's using, she's nearly impossible." Her eyes were distant and sad.

My gut squeezed to think these people once had a baby just like Elsie, and now they had tears in their eyes over their grown child. Their deeply troubled child who sacrificed her own baby because deep in her heart she knew she wasn't the person to raise Elsie.

No one knew the future.

No one expected their child to turn to drugs.

To lash out, to take risks to dull the pain.

To make every single interaction one of rage and hate.

I didn't know what had happened between Carl, Lea, and Sasha all those years ago.

But my heart hurt to think Elsie would ever become a person we didn't know anymore. A person it was painful to be around.

Carl picked up the story. "During an argument as we sipped our coffee and tried to pretend we were a happy family, Sasha let it slip that she'd had a baby."

Lea drew in a shuddery breath. "I knew she said it to hurt us, and I just waited for her to go in for the kill." She shook her head. "Then she said, 'I signed away my rights so Elsie wouldn't grow up with a mom like me. I saved her from that. Saved her from what I went through.'"

Carl held his head in his hands. "We weren't the best parents. There's no arguing that. But Sasha was a... difficult...child from the day we brought her home. No amount of therapy or medication or in-patient rehab ever reached her."

Silence filled the room, broken only by a cooing noise from Elsie.

Lea's tears finally spilled over and she held her hand to her mouth. "We were hurt and confused after Sasha told us about the baby. We acted without thinking and we are so very sorry. There will never be a day we don't regret any heartache we might have caused."

Beside me, Colby had relaxed bit by bit as the Klein's told their story. I had a feeling he understood where they were coming from after surviving his mom, Mandy, and Sasha being such traumatic parts of his life.

"We reached out to the first attorney we found on the internet," Carl said, his face pinking. "As my wife said, we were hurt and not thinking clearly. We wanted information about where things stood, if we had any legal right to see the baby."

Lea, tears streaming freely now, shook her head. "We had *no* idea that man would send the letter without our consent. When he called us the next day and told us what he'd done—"

"'Just to grease the wheels a bit he said. Get things moving in the right direction. Throw them off so they see things our way.'" Carl grimaced.

"He acted as if we'd be *happy* about what he'd done.

Gave us some big runaround about how he'd never had clients be so ungrateful and how we'd be singing his praises when he got us full custody." Lea cursed. "By that point, we'd had time to reevaluate and look into Earnst. We figured out quickly that he's a dirtbag."

"I assure you, we've hired an actual attorney to look into bringing suit against him," Carl added.

"It took us a bit of digging to figure out where you lived," Lea went on. "We could have asked Earnst since he'd clearly found you with no problem, but turning to him for help with anything felt like adding insult to injury. Once we found your location, we had to make travel arrangements; we live overseas, so it wasn't just a quick trip."

"What happened is such a regretful mistake," Carl said. "The timing is horrific and the fear it must have caused you is unforgivable."

"We never wanted full custody of Elsie," Lea said, her arms tucked protectively around her middle. "We didn't want *any* custody to be honest. We're too old to care for a baby." She let her husband take her hand. "I think we just wanted to know if we had the right to ask to see her or get pictures. Then that man went and sent that letter to you." She wiped a tear. "I have never been more ashamed and angry at something in my life."

Colby cleared his throat. "Thank you for setting things straight." He took my hand. If Carl or Lea were shocked or bothered, they didn't let on. "It's been hell since we got that letter—and I'm pretty sure our own attorney will have a ball going after Mr. Earnst—but it helps to know you aren't trying to take her from us."

"We aren't," Lea said. "Not at all."

Colby glanced my way and I knew what he was about to say nearly killed him, but the determined glint in his eye told me there was nothing going to stop him. He took a deep breath and held his arms out for Elsie.

She grinned, slobbery and happy, and lunged for him.

Colby pressed his head to Elsie's and closed his eyes before kissing her forehead. "Would you—" he started, but had to stop, the words caught in his throat. "Would you like to hold her?"

Lea's eyes flew to him. "I—" she started, as if she thought she needed to say no. "I'd be delighted. Thank you."

Colby stood and moved toward Lea. Placing Elsie in the older woman's arms, he knelt down beside them. Perfect protective position, plus it allowed Elsie to see him.

"Oh, my goodness," Lea breathed. "She looks so much like Sasha."

"Would it be possible," Carl started, but paused to clear his throat. "Would it be possible to get pictures of her from time to time?"

Colby and I nodded at the same time.

These people had made a mistake and been taken advantage of, but I couldn't find it in my heart to deprive them of watching Elsie grow up.

"I'd like very much if we could send her letters. You can keep them for her. When she's an adult, she can read them. If she'd like to contact us, she can," Lea said.

"Let us have some time to think it over," Colby said. "But maybe we can get one of those electronic picture frames. We can send pictures to you and maybe you can send pictures to us. I don't think letting her know her grandparents is a bad thing." He frowned. "I'd just like to keep her away from Sasha—at least until she's an adult. Once she's grown, if she wants to meet her mother, that will be her choice."

Carl and Lea nodded, tears streaking down their cheeks.

"Thank you," Lea whispered before pressing a kiss to Elsie's head. "This is so much more than we deserve after everything."

Colby shook his head. "I know what's it like to have bad shit happen. I don't think you purposely set out to hurt us. If our baby has more people to love and support her, I can't see keeping that from her." He turned to Carl. "Would you like to hold her?"

An hour later, we exchanged email addresses and teary hugs while Elsie clapped and squealed, oblivious to her daddies miraculously avoiding potentially disastrous drama in her little life.

When the door closed behind the Kleins, Colby yanked me close and sobbed into my chest, Elsie pinned gently between us. I let the tears flow and kissed Elsie's cheek before resting my lips against Colby's head.

Elsie blew a raspberry and patted us both on the head. "Dadda."

Eyes wide, tears and snot flowing, Colby and I jerked our heads apart and looked at our daughter.

"Did she just say…" I asked.

Elsie, tucked against Colby's side, flailed her arms, smacking us both in the face. "Dadda."

Best.

Christmas.

Ever.

Christmas Eve lunch was spent with the guys.

Emory and Ivy brought Magic and Elsie patted the dog's head. "Maj." Not spot-on, but close enough. She spent the rest of the day babbling *dadda* and *Maj*, her gummy grin delighting everyone.

Based on the increased drool, and information we'd gleaned from our book and the parenting blog, she'd be trying to pop some teeth through sooner rather than later. Hopefully, Santa would be bringing plenty of baby Tylenol.

Christmas Eve evening was spent gathered around the tree with our parents, the fireplace roaring, and Elsie babbling. The only two words that sounded like anything continued to be *dadda* and *Maj*, but the adults doted on her and hung on every single syllable.

By Christmas morning, the fear had eased, replaced by gut-deep relief. Elsie was *our* daughter, and she was safe and happy with us. No one was trying to take her away. The mental and emotional exhaustion of the past several days had taken their toll, but we were together. Our little family was safe.

"She'll be out for another hour," Colby whispered at my ear while rocking his morning erection against my ass. "Can you be quiet?"

We'd slowly been moving Elsie's bed farther from ours with the goal to move it to her room once she'd mastered napping in there during the day. To be honest, she was doing great with naps in her own room, it was her daddies who weren't doing so well with moving her out of our room.

"Get the lube."

As quietly as possible, we shucked our underwear and slicked ourselves in the still-dark morning. Stifling a groan when Colby worked a finger into me, I quickly doubted my ability to keep quiet once he got his dick in me.

"Shhh," he breathed at my ear. "You're gonna take this cock and not make a peep. If we wake her up, we'll spend Christmas Day with blue balls." He gripped my chin and turned me for a kiss. "Can you do it?"

I melted into the kiss and nodded. "Go slow."

Colby pressed into me inch by inch, my body opening for him, stretching around the thick invasion, pleasure coursing through my veins. With my face buried in a pillow, I kept my whimpers and moans to a minimum with each and every slide of Colby's cock in and out of my hole.

When he stilled his thrusting, I bit my lip to keep from crying out as his hot release spilled deep inside me. Colby slipped from my body much too soon, but he turned me to my back and took my throbbing cock between his lips. Eyes staring up at me, barely visible as the first hint of sunlight peeked through the windows, he sucked me. Playing with my balls and finger fucking his cum back into me, Colby worked me into a frenzy. Only one tiny cry of pleasure escaped me when I unloaded down his throat, but we'd barely had time to recover when Elsie started her squirmy, grunty wake-up noises.

"Merry Christmas," Colby whispered when he'd kissed his way up my body. "I love you."

"Love you," I murmured against his lips. "Merry Christmas."

An hour later, we were showered and dressed. The tree glowed brightly as if to say *This is it, this is my day.* The three ornaments seemed to sparkle and gleam more than ever, and I couldn't help but wonder if maybe there really was something to the Christmas magic Emory went on and on about.

Breakfast and coffee were first on our list.

"Next year maybe, definitely the next, she'll be too excited for us to get coffee before gifts, better enjoy it now," Colby said, and I knew he wasn't wrong.

Once Elsie had eaten breakfast, we helped her open some gifts and laughed at the fact she most definitely was more interested in the paper and boxes than the toys.

"What's that one?" I asked, pointing to a gift under the tree I hadn't seen before that exact moment.

Colby shrugged. "Hmm, don't know. Thought you put it there. Open it."

My eyes narrowed at his nonchalance, but I grabbed the package and settled in next to him. "I thought we agreed no gifts this year? All of *this*," I gestured around the room, "is enough."

"Just open it," he urged.

The sound of paper tearing caught Elsie's attention and if she'd been able to crawl yet, she would have made a beeline.

The ornate wooden sign nestled in the tissue paper was absolutely gorgeous. It matched the wood in our living room and dining room perfectly, but the words had my heart caught in my throat.

Jackson-Burke

Party of Three

My eyes flew to Colby only to find him on his damn knee with a ring. He shrugged. "I went with Jackson-Burke so she doesn't get made fun of."

I scowled. "What?"

"Elsie Mae Burke-Jackson could be shortened to Elsie Mae B-J and no one wants BJ in their name."

I laughed through the sting of tears.

"We don't have to do it right now. Don't have to do it big or fancy." Colby took my hand and caressed my knuckles. "But we made a deal way back when and I'll be damned if I'm not going to stick to it." He slipped the simple black band onto my left hand. "Kai David Jackson, will you marry me? You know, since we're thirty and single?"

I fell into his arms, toppling the two of us into the pile of wrapping paper. The kiss was long and sensual. When we finally broke apart, Elsie was on her hands and knees looking as if she was going to crawl in mere moments.

We held our breaths.

And…

She fell to the floor, bumped her chin, and burst into tears.

Colby and I broke apart, hurrying into daddy-duty. I grabbed Elsie and he started throwing away the wrapping paper.

"Wait, even if we don't do it right now…" I took his hand and brought it to my mouth for a kiss. "I want you to have a ring too."

Colby grimaced. "Oops, forgot that part." He reached into his pocket and produced a matching ring.

I snatched the ring from his fingers and pulled him

close. "I'm not going to saddle our daughter with a name like Elsie Mae CoJack," I said as I slipped the ring onto his finger, "but just know, married or not, we will always be CoJack."

"Forever," he answered before kissing me.

Later, as Elsie played with a bow while surrounded by all her new toys, my phone rang. Ivy and Emory did a video call to wish us Merry Christmas. Ivy panned the living room asking us if The Creeps looked even creepier. Emory babbled away about the snow globe, but it didn't take him long to catch the rings on our fingers. I swear the whole neighborhood heard him scream.

Once Ivy had his man settled down a bit, we let Elsie *talk* to her besties. But she wasn't terribly interested in the video version of Magic, so we made plans to see them later that day or the next.

"Like you'd be able to keep me away." Emory held his hands to his cheeks with a tiny squeal. "Oh my god, we're going to have a wedding!"

After the call, we just sat close and absorbed all the goodness of the moment. "Do you ever wish our house had all the Christmas magic like Ivy and Em?" I asked over the rim of my coffee cup while Colby took a wet piece of wrapping paper from Elsie's chubby little fist.

He sat back against the couch with me. "Nah, the stockings showing up was plenty for me. Plus, we don't need Christmas magic. Look at our daughter." Colby took my hand and squeezed before tracing his thumb over the metal band around my finger. Elsie's eyes sparkled in the light from the tree. "Seeing Christmas through her eyes, being with you, families and friends nearby, that's the only magic I need."

The three ornaments caught my eye again and I smiled. Whether it was a touch of Christmas magic or just the love burning bright between us, I wouldn't trade it for all the money in the world.

Leaning my head on Colby's shoulder while Elsie chanted *dadadada* over and over, I hummed appreciatively. "Yeah, couldn't ask for anything more. What we have is absolutely perfect."

EPILOGUE
COLBY

Christmas Morning – One Year Later

We lay plastered together, our breaths coming hard and heavy as we came down from earth-shattering orgasms. We'd quickly discovered that moving Elsie to her own room, locking our door, and keeping the monitor close by had been the perfect combination when it came to sexy time for dads of a toddler.

"I say she's awake in under ten minutes," Kai mumbled against my arm.

"Or less. She was hyped about Santa last night."

Elsie was just under a year and a half. She'd hit pretty much every single milestone and flew past them with flying colors. Our little girl was a talker, curious almost to a fault, and had a creative streak we planned to nurture.

She didn't completely get the whole idea of Santa—and let's be honest, it's not exactly an easy thing to wrap your brain around seeing as how it's pretty much just a lie, but I digress...but on Christmas Eve she'd eaten too many of Emory's cookies, laughed herself silly with her best buddy

Magic, and chattered the entire way home about Ho-Ho coming to her house.

As if on cue, Elsie started gabbing to herself as she did most mornings. She could climb out of her bed, but she usually stayed put as long as we got to her fairly quickly.

"Dada!"

Kai smiled against my arm.

"Da-dee!"

God, what that baby girl could do to my heart.

We rolled out of bed, and wiped ourselves down knowing we'd have to shower quickly later so we weren't late for the big day.

With Kai taking care of a quick diaper change, I made my way downstairs to make sure the living room was set up perfectly. We'd gone with the same decorations as last year. Those damn stockings had disappeared the day after Christmas and shown up out of nowhere again this year. When one lived in Peppermint Hollow, one learned to just take shit like that with the flow.

When I suggested maybe we should try to find more round ornaments to match the three we had, Kai was adamant we keep them the same. "They're the three of us. A touch of magic or not, they're perfect. If we want a different theme, we can do another tree. Maybe in the dining room; a bit more formal if you want."

I'd kissed him and told him our tree was perfect, just like our little family.

We'd continued reading parenting articles online and recently they'd come through for us with gift suggestions for kids Elsie's age for Christmas. She absolutely loved the books, the wobble rocker toy, and the wooden garden shape sorter we got her.

We took pictures and sent them to Carl and Lea before struggling through breakfast with a toddler who would rather play than eat.

Things with Sasha's parents had been easy and good. We sent them pictures on a fun little digital frame at least once a month. They mailed letters and cards to Elsie for us to keep in a safe place until she was older. About every other month, an outfit and a toy would show up at the house, and we'd video call them so they could see Elsie in the clothes and playing with the toy. They were good people, despite the screw-up, and I didn't regret them getting to know Elsie.

Sasha hadn't made a peep. Part of me feared she'd gone too far and hadn't been able to make it back from the edge this time. The other part figured she was just too caught up in her own survival to worry about Elsie. Sometimes that made me angry, but mostly I appreciated Sasha's understanding of herself and her troubles to give Elsie to me before anything got ugly.

Our attorney and the Klein's attorney had both filed suit against Frederick Earnst. There had been enough complaints against him that an official investigation had been opened. The situation wouldn't be resolved for quite some time, but Earnst had lost his license, already paid some hefty fines, and would spend the next few years drowning in lawsuits and court cases.

"I still can't believe they decided to get married on Christmas day," Kai said later that morning as he donned his tie in front of the mirror in the dining room.

Elsie screamed and ran in circles in her pretty flower girl dress as I shrugged into my suit jacket.

"I mean, I know *we* opted for a Friday at the

courthouse, but that was because we wanted the reception to be Saturday with all our friends," he went on. "Plus, we picked a nice fall day with pretty leaves and decent temps."

"It *was* a really nice wedding," I said, recalling our short and sweet ceremony surrounded by our parents and friends. We'd exchanged vows and promised to love each other forever—as if we hadn't known we'd do that with or without rings and a piece of paper.

"We did a good job," Kai said with a smile before kissing me. "I'm sure today will be just as nice. Colder, but nice."

"It's their day and we just need to be there for them," I said even though I wasn't sure I'd want to get married in the snow.

Trevor and Blake had opted for a tiny wedding in their backyard. Trevor had moved into Blake's house over the summer, and their decision to get married had come quickly, but not as a surprise.

"I'm just shocked they beat Ivy and Emory to it," Kai said.

"Ivy for sure won't be doing anything anyone expects."

Snatching Elsie up, we worked to get her into a little fur stole that matched her dress, the latch silver just like her shoes.

Once out the back door, I couldn't help the sad, fond smile as I let my eyes wander to Francis's old home. Our backyard neighbor hadn't returned from his niece's last year. She'd contacted us to let us know Francis had passed peacefully in his sleep.

"He spoke so very highly of you both," she'd said when

she called. "He was so happy to know you ended up together. I know he's with his dear Sammy now."

Francis had left a sizeable sum of money to his niece's children and Elsie in his will. *That beautiful girl with the two amazing daddies will one day take on the world. I know she'll do great things and I know CoJack will be there watching every step of the way.*

The family who'd moved into Francis's house were colleagues of Blake's at the physical therapy center. Their son, Zechariah, was just a few months older than Elsie. He was the ring bearer in the wedding.

Emory had deemed Elsie and Zechariah the next great love story.

"They'll be playmates. They'll grow up together, get married, have babies."

Ivy had laughed at my frown over that part.

"And they'll name their little boy Garrison after his grandpa Colby, and their little girl will be named Ivy since Elsie is Ivy's biggest fan."

It was true, aside from Elsie's love of Magic and her daddies, she thought the sun rose and set on Ivy. It was cute how Emory and Elsie shared the same abject adoration for the guy.

Over the next hour, our tiny group of friends and family gathered under outdoor heaters to witness Blake and Trevor pledge their lives to each other as big, fluffy flakes of snow danced through the crisp, cold air.

Elsie, Zechariah, and Magic were all absolutely adorable as they made their way down the makeshift aisle.

Trevor and Blake would have made a heart of ice melt as they swore to love each other until the end of time.

When a chorus of tiny bells rang out, Emory snuggled closer to Ivy and mouthed, "Magic," to me.

No bells were to be seen but they made their music all the same, and snow fell to blanket the ground like the most perfect made-for-TV holiday romance.

Kai knelt next to Elsie and handed her an envelope. "Wanna give this to Dada?"

I dropped to a crouch and held my arms out for Elsie as she beelined toward me. "What's this?" I asked in the voice I reserved just for her. "Is it from Daddy?" Elsie giggled and flailed the envelope.

With my eyes locked on my husband, his lip caught between his teeth, I tore into the envelope. I scanned the paper once.

Twice.

As my eyes filled with tears, I read it a third time.

"Is this…" My words caught.

Emory, Ivy, Blake, and Trevor stood behind Kai. Our parents stood next to me. Elsie kissed Magic's head between us.

"It's a petition to file for adoption," Kai answered. "I want it official if it's okay with you."

I scooped Elsie up and took a step to pull Kai in for a long kiss. "She's been yours since the first time you held her and nothing will ever change that. But I want it on paper that she's legally Elsie Mae Jackson-Burke."

We pressed kisses to Elsie's pretty little head, laughing when she squealed and wanted down. Second place to Magic, as usual.

"Maybe it's just a touch of magic," Kai murmured as we watched our daughter lift her face to the sky and stick out her tongue. Tiny snow crystals caught on her thick, black lashes, and Magic chomped at falling flakes by her side.

I pressed a kiss to his temple, my heart a full three sizes too big with love for my daughter and my Kai. "Maybe, but who needs magic when we've got CoJack?"

"Forever."

~The End~

Read on for extra scenes from Colby and Kai's love story.

THE WEDDING

COLBY BURKE

ELSIE MAE PLAYED PATTY-CAKE WITH MY CHEEKS as the late afternoon sun filtered through the Wintergreen County courthouse windows. The building had been built before my parents were born. It smelled old. Papers, book glue, old wood all combined to create a musty scent I thought I'd likely recognize anywhere.

In addition to smelling old, the courthouse looked old with its marble floors and columns, like something that would have easily fit into an old black and white holiday movie.

But with the autumn leaves flashing red, gold, and orange on the soft breeze blowing outside the judge's window, this particular old, musty courthouse was setting up to be the location of one of my very favorite memories ever.

Today was the day.

I'd loved Kai in one way or another since we were just kids. I'd inched closer and closer to falling for him with each step we took toward the precipice of adulthood all those years ago. For years, he'd stood by me while I fought my demons—patient, supportive, the other half to my whole.

And then he'd blown my damn mind by stepping up for Elsie and me when I found myself floundering as a brand new single father.

All the years between our bumbling teen years and Kai coming to California to rescue me had shown me that my best friend was loyal, caring, and dedicated to what we had—even when what we had was just friendship.

Kai was my forever whether we were just friends or more.

Thank god we'd figured out we wanted to be more.

And today I got to officially call my best friend my husband.

Didn't matter that neither of us really cared for the fact the government had to be involved with our vows to love each other forever.

Didn't matter that it had taken a ridiculous teenage bet called in when we were thirty and single to get to this point.

Didn't matter that we'd opted for a small wedding at the county courthouse on a beautiful Friday afternoon in the fall with our family and friends.

Hell, it didn't actually even matter if Kai and I skipped the whole marriage license and hyphenating our last names.

We'd loved each other our entire lives. No piece of paper, no officiant, and no hyphen were going to change that. Kai and I had been joined at the hip—each of us the floundering half to our whole—for what seemed like eternity.

If other lifetimes existed, I had no doubt Kai and I were soulmates who would travel through as many lives as we were given if it meant finding each other time and time again.

Today, I was marrying the man I loved, my best friend, and the father of my baby girl.

"You ready?" Dad asked as Allison took Elsie Mae from me. My baby girl was dressed in the sweetest little red, yellow, and orange sweater dress with adorable brown suede boots.

Straightening my olive green bomber jacket over the cream henley, I took a deep breath and rubbed my hands on the thighs of my stylishly ripped black jeans. We hadn't seen each other's outfits yet, but I knew Kai wouldn't be surprised by my favorite black boots.

"I am," I said, my words confident and strong.

Dad pulled me into a hug and slapped me on the back. "Glad I get to be here for this. You two deserve all the happiness in the world."

"Thank you." The words caught in my throat. "Back then, I never dreamed any of us would make it to this point, but there's no place I'd rathe be."

"I'm sorry—"

"Dad, don't. It's in the past. We're so much better than good now."

He cleared his throat. "Just want you to know how damn proud I am of you and the man you've become. I'm damn lucky to have you and Kai as my sons, and maybe I'm biased, but I have the best granddaughter in the whole world."

Emotions threatened to spill over, so I just hugged my dad again. "She is pretty great."

A knock sounded at the door, and Kai's dad peeked his head around. "There's my favorite son-in-law." I chuckled as my future father-in-law winked. Eric's dad jokes were one of the things I loved about the man. Would Kai eventually be a middle-aged dad telling jokes? Yeah. No question, he definitely would. "You ready to do this?"

I nodded.

Eric threw an arm around my shoulders and pulled me into a hug. "Glad you two have always had each other. Thanks to your friendship, we've got one big happy family. You're good for him in ways I don't know he even realizes."

Clearing my throat, I slapped him on the back. "He's the one who's good for me. He's kept me going during times I didn't think I was going to make it through."

"Like I said, glad you've got each other." Eric ended the embrace, shook my dad's hand—which ended up in a good ol' fashioned back slapping bro hug.

They left the little room a few minutes later, and I stood alone by the window for a silent moment. The sun on my face, the fall leaves swirling in the wind, and two rings promising forever clinking in my pocket.

My messed up past—from the shit with my mom, the absence of my dad, and two majorly failed relationships—didn't stand a chance today. Kai had saved me when I needed him the most. He'd always been there, but he'd been my lifeline when Elsie was born. And I wanted to remember the day I got to make him mine forever and always.

Taking a deep breath, I checked my pocket again for the rings we'd picked out together, and walked toward the judge's chambers.

Because we wanted something simple and quick, we'd only invited our friends and family. But we'd also wanted to write our own vows and not see each other until the moment we both entered the chambers.

Tears of happiness mixed with disbelief when I saw everyone crowded into the small space. Dad, Allison, Eric, Lacy—who was holding a giggling Elsie Mae—Ivy and Emory, Trevor and Blake, the judge and her clerk. How was I so lucky to have this many people loving and supporting me? Helping me raise my daughter. Standing behind Kai and me through thick and thin.

Aside from my own father—who'd left me wondering at times if he'd ever really and truly be able to be what we both needed him to be—all of these people were my family by choice. Even Dad, to some extent, because I chose to work things through with him and give him a second chance.

I didn't *have* to love Allison and Lacy like the mothers I never really had.

Eric's friendship had been a guiding light for both me and my dad over the years, and I appreciated the man's steady place in our lives.

Ivy, Emory, Trevor, and Blake. Four men I never would have met had Kai not convinced me to return to Peppermint Hollow. The thought of life without them in it wasn't one I could even fathom. They were my friends, my brothers, my safe space. They were a bunch of knuckle heads. They could be loud, obnoxious, and raunchy as hell —okay, that was mostly Ivy, but still. They were also a sounding board, a shoulder to lean on, and a listening ear.

If anyone ever said *found family* wasn't real, I'd show them the family I'd surrounded myself with. These people who'd shown up for me, loved me without trying to change me, and wanted nothing but the best for me. They were my family. Period.

As I walked toward the front of the room, Elsie caught sight of me and shrieked. Lunging from Lacy's arms, she almost took the petite woman down. Laughing, I grabbed my baby and whirled her into a hug.

"Hey, Els, you ready to see your daddies get married?" I peppered kisses over her cheeks while she giggled hysterically.

The door to the right opened just as the judge moved to stand front and center before her bench. Kai, dressed in a casual sweater of rust and cream, brown jeans, and soft brown loafers, popped his head around the doorway with a grin. "This the right place?"

Elsie giggled and babbled, "Dada!"

I turned to hand our daughter back to Lacy, but Elsie started to cry. Kai made a beeline toward me and took her in his arms. "Let's do this, Elsie Mae." He grabbed my hand and hauled me toward the judge. "We're ready."

I snorted.

Kai bumped me with his elbow before leaning in to whisper, "You look gorgeous. Love you." The kiss he feathered over my cheek warmed me from head to toe.

"Love you," I said back, squeezing his hand.

The judge smiled. "Well, gentlemen, this is definitely the best part of my job. Let's get this baby's daddies married."

Most of the short and sweet ceremony was likely lost to me forever no matter how badly I wanted to lock every word into my memory and savor it for years to come.

But our vows?

Our vows would stick with me forever.

Partly because each word Kai spoke to me felt as if it were being etched into the very fabric of my soul.

Also because Allison and Lacy had already promised to get our vows printed and framed.

And thank goodness for video.

With Elsie propped on his hip, Kai kept hold of my hand as he faced me. He took a deep breath and huffed out a laugh. "These are on a card in my pocket, but Miss Priss is blocking my access. Let's see if I can wing it."

Tears threatened, and he hadn't even said a single sappy word. I was toast.

Kai cleared his throat. "Colby…" He swallowed, and the tears sparkling in his eyes caught me right in the heart. He breathed in deeply through his nose and gave me that heart-melting grin I'd come to love so much. Shaking away the emotion, he continued, "You've been my best friend from the very beginning. We've been through a lot, but the one thing that never changed was that we loved each other and supported each other through it all."

I squeezed his hand, a lump forming in my throat watching him get choked up. This man—the love of my life before I even knew what love truly was—holding our daughter as he fought off tears and pledged to spend the rest of his life with me was all too much.

Kai chuckled when we both wiped away tears.

"All I ever wanted was to see you happy," he went on. "But selfishly, I also never wanted you happy with anyone but me. I'm the worst." Another tear fell, and I reached to thumb it from his cheek.

By this time, Elsie was watching us intently, focused

on whether or not she should be concerned at the way her daddies were acting.

"I promised myself I'd be okay with us just being friends," he said with a snort. "We'd made it this long, I could make it work." Kai pressed a kiss to Elsie's head. "And then my entire world shifted because you loved me right back. Not just like we'd always loved each other, but the way I'd dreamed of you loving me since I was a kid."

I handed him the ring from my pocket. Tears streamed down Kai's face as he slipped the thin metal band onto my finger.

"Colby Burke, you are my dream come true. I vow to love you forever and always, to raise our daughter with you, and to cherish our friendship." He pulled my hand to his lips and pressed a kiss to my knuckles. "CoJack forever," he whispered.

The only sounds in the courtroom were sniffs and throats clearing, and I chuckled. "I knew I should have gone first."

That got a couple laughs, but Elsie startled and started to cry. Judge Watson hurried to hush her, and Elsie let the older woman take her from Kai's arms. Our baby was immediately intrigued with the sparkly chain attached to the judge's glasses, and for a moment, her attention was focused elsewhere.

"Kai," I started, but stopped when the words didn't want to come out. Closing my eyes, I took a cleansing breath, and then locked gazes with the man who held my soul. "There was never a question of me loving you. I just took an extra long journey to reach the point where I could recognize what we had."

"To BFE and back. Twice," Kai mumbled with a grin.

Laughter bubbled from me, and I wiped away the tears. "Yeah, well, no one ever accused me of doing things the easy way." I shook my head as our guests laughed. "You've been my rock, my everything, for as long as I could remember. When I think about the times in my life when I was the most lost, it's always when I wasn't with you."

Kai blinked rapidly and pressed his lips together.

"One of the worst periods in my life led me to the two most absolutely perfect moments—when our daughter was born, and when I heard you tell her you were in love with me." I pulled the ring from my pocket and slid it onto Kai's finger. "I vow to love you for eternity, in this lifetime and the next. I vow to support you, I vow to let you decorate the Christmas tree however you want." The laughter I heard was definitely from Ivy and Emory. "And I vow to stand by your side through anything and everything this life wants to throw at us." Pulling his hand to my mouth, I feathered kisses over his knuckles. "CoJack forever."

THE RECEPTION

KAI JACKSON-BURKE

"Thank you for being here," I said to the crowd. "Enjoy the food and drinks while we do some pictures and cut the cake."

The Peppermint Hollow community center contained several rooms for gathering large groups of people, and the one we'd rented for the day after our wedding was full of friends, family, colleagues, neighbors, and folks from around town who knew me and Colby or our parents.

We'd dressed a bit more casually than we had for the ceremony in jeans, sweaters, and fashion sneakers. We'd opted for a navy blue, gray, and gold color scheme to blend with the fall decor, but we hadn't wanted to get too dressy. Colby and I were the most comfortable with each other in our favorite clothes, so it didn't make sense to us to get all glammed up just because we were taking pictures.

Elsie Mae looked absolutely ridiculously cute in her navy blue, gray, and gold flannel shirt dress, navy tights, soft gold boots, and bows of navy and gold in her hair.

While our guests mingled, made up plates of food--which we'd had catered from local businesses—and got drinks at the open bar, Colby and I let the photographer position us in about a million locations for pictures. Some of us alone, most with Elsie Mae while she was cooperating, and many with our parents and friends.

"Let's get photos of you guys cutting the cake," the photographer said. "Then I'll just spend the rest of my time taking candids."

Our cake was a chocolate-vanilla marble layer cake with rich, creamy chocolate ganache and vanilla buttercream separating the layers. The fondant was a dark chocolate decorated with navy blue, gray, and gold swirls, and accented with colorful fall fondant leaves. We'd skipped the traditional topper because we couldn't find one we loved and opted to replace it with a miniature bouquet of navy blue, gray, and gold flowers, leaves, and ribbons.

By the time we'd done the cake cutting pictures—and cleaned the frosting from our faces because of course we had to smash cake into each other's mouth—the DJ had started the music.

"I'm fucking starving," Colby said as he took my hand and led me toward the food. "We have to eat before we do anything else."

He got absolutely no argument from me.

We loaded our plates and moved to sit at the little table reserved for us as Elsie ran in circles shrieking on the dance floor.

When we'd filled our bellies sufficiently enough to make it through the rest of the party, I noticed Emory talking to the DJ.

"What's he up to?"

Colby's eyes followed my gaze. "No telling with Em."

Ivy joined Emory, said a few words, and then the two of them moved toward the middle of the dance floor with a microphone.

Trevor and Blake joined them.

Ivy tapped on the microphone. "Testing, testing. This thing on?"

His words stopped Elsie in her tracks and she made a beeline for him. Ivy didn't even blink these days when his miniature best friend came running for him. He handed the mic to Emory, gathered Elsie up in his arms, and then took the mic back.

"So, Colby and Kai didn't ask us to be best men or make speeches or anything," he started in that wry Ivy way.

"Rude," Emory, Trevor, and Blake chorused.

Colby put his hand on my leg as we both prepared for whatever our best friends had schemed up.

"Instead of making speeches summing up all the great—"

"And not so great," Emory chimed in with a grin.

Ivy smiled. "And not so great things about Mr. and Mr. Jackson-Burke…" He paused for the applause, and then he had to wait for Elsie to stop clapping and blowing raspberries right in his face. "Thanks, Els," he said with a huff, but the love and adoration he had for our little girl was evident in Ivy's every move. "Instead of the usual speeches, we decided we'd do some karaoke. We've put together a list of songs we think represent Colby and Kai's love story pretty well. Performers can choose from our list, or pick one of their own."

With that, Dad and Tom rolled in a huge karaoke machine as our guests cheered. Who knew Peppermint Hollow was so eager for some karaoke action?

It was likely the free booze pouring.

"Glad we decided to shut down the bar a couple hours before the party ends," Colby whispered as the crowd split to get drinks or pick their song.

"Yeah, and it's good most everyone walked here." I watched in fascination as a mixed group of people poured over the song sheet the guys had put together or flipped through the binder of pre-programmed songs that came with the machine. "I can't believe this many people want to sing. Did the guys pay them?"

Colby snorted and shrugged. "Must be something missing in our little town. All the talk of Christmas magic, but who knew what the good folk really wanted was a karaoke night."

The evening played out in front of us like a dream we didn't even know we needed. Friends, family, and people we'd know since we were kids took turns singing a variety of songs—some emotional and sentimental, some silly and fun, and everything in between.

People sang, we all danced, and it was the perfect celebration of what Colby and I had found in each other.

Ivy, Emory, Trevor, and Blake shocked the shit out of us when they did a surprisingly good rendition of Home by Phillip Phillips before launching into a hilarious and only slightly raunchy version of Troublemaker by Olly Murs and Flo Rida.

Mom and Allison blew us away with their performance of I Will Wait by Mumford & Sons.

But the highlight of the evening was when Dad and

Tom took the stage. "This song was popular when we were teens," Dad explained.

"We think it fits what you two are for each other," Tom added.

And then they proceeded to kill it on the song I'll Be Your Everything by Tommy Page. Granted, I didn't know the song, and I had to look it up, but our dads absolutely slayed.

But then Ivy, who had been dancing Elsie around the whole time, handed her off to Emory. "Now comes the time of our party for the new husbands to share a dance. I think they have a song picked out."

At least this part we'd planned for.

Colby stood and took my hand. He walked us to Ivy and took the mic. Just when I thought he'd tell the DJ to play our song, he squeezed my hand and put the mic to his mouth.

"Back in high school, this song played at our Winter Ball. Twice. A lot of our history is private just for me and Kai, but we both listened to this song about five billion times over the years. There are so many things in these lyrics that fit us perfectly. We took our sweet time getting to this point, but it wasn't wasted because we've always had each other." He nodded toward the DJ, and music flowed from the speakers. "If you know it, sing along while I dance with my husband and best friend."

The guests clapped. Ivy took the mic. My eyes stung. And Colby wrapped me in his arms as I Won't Give Up by Jason Mraz filled the air.

"You are soooo getting laid tonight," I whispered at Colby's ear before pressing a kiss to his temple.

Colby chuckled. "Good to know since I was thinking the same thing."

"Guess we're lucky Elsie's with my parents tonight."

We swayed to the music, our bodies perfectly slotted together, as visions of what we might get up to with a whole child-free night sent heat straight to my balls.

"Mmhm," Colby hummed, his hand pressed against my lower back. "Are we dumb for not taking a honeymoon?"

"Nope." I kissed him as our friends and family sang around us. "We know what we want. Next summer, when Elsie can appreciate the beach, the characters, and the rides, we'll head to the happiest place on earth with our friends and family."

The song started again, and our tipsy guests sang with much more gusto, but they also paired off or formed small groups to dance around us.

"I love you so damn much." Colby's strangled whisper and the way he fisted my sweater heated my blood and had me wanting to skip the rest of the reception. "Thank you for being patient and never giving up on me."

"I love you," I murmured at his ear. "I'm the luckiest man alive to call you my husband *and* my best friend."

"CoJack," Colby mouthed at my temple, the single word sending shivers through me.

"Forever," we whispered in unison.

And then Elsie shrieked and ran toward us. Colby picked up our little girl, and the three of us danced around like fools with our friends and family.

Not everyone got to live the life of their dreams with the person they loved, and I wasn't going to waste a single second of it.

Have you read Ivy and Emory's story in Once Upon a Christmas House? Find it on ebook, audio, and paperback on Amazon. Also available in a signed paperback version on my webstore (https://payhip.com/ADEllisAuthor)

ALSO BY A.D. ELLIS

Jett & Leighton: On Cravenwood Block- a steamy, opposites-attract, bisexual-awakening, roommates-to-lovers M/M romance featuring a sexy-as-sin tattoo artist and a fresh, flashy barista with a smile that lights up the room.

Ollie & Bash: On Cravenwood Block- a steamy, opposites-attract, roommates-to-lovers, boss/employee, age-gap M/M romance featuring a man not looking for love and a younger music director with no filter.

Julian & Shaw: On Cravenwood Block- a steamy, hurt/comfort, roommates-to-lovers, age-gap M/M romance featuring an apartment manager with a heart of gold and a younger man doing his best to heal from a traumatic past.

Holly Hills Christmas- Holly Hills Christmas is a steamy, feel-good, M/M age-gap holiday romance.

The Perfect Blend- A steamy, M/M age-gap, marriage of convenience, coffee shop romance

Perfect Timing is a steamy, M/M romance with an introverted, demisexual writer and a big, soft teddy bear of a nurse trying to navigate a love they've always dreamed of but most definitely weren't expecting.

Adore (Remington Place 1) is a steamy, age-gap, bi-awakening, dad's best friend M/M romance with a sassy smartass and a sexy silver fox. It's the first book in the Remington Place series and can be read as a stand-alone.

Crave (Remington Place 2) is a steamy, friends-to-lovers, fake relationship M/M romance with a virgin nursing student and a gruff, grumbly construction worker.

Desire (Remington Place 3) is a steamy, age-gap, hurt/comfort

M/M romance featuring a heart-of-gold mechanic and a twink who's a lot stronger than he realizes. *Please note: This story has mention of sex trafficking and sexual abuse.*

Yearn (Remington Place 4)- a steamy, enemies-to-lovers, forced proximity M/M romance between two EMS workers who have hated each other for a decade.

Power Struggle is a steamy M/M, age-gap, forced proximity romance set in a small town. A twenty-year history, rival schools and jobs, and a hotel with only one bed make for a hot and heavy, sweet and sexy, HEA-guaranteed love story.

Take Me Home M/M age-gap, opposites-attract romance with plenty of steam and a scene that will make you appreciate camouflage and work boots

Let Love In M/M age-gap, forced proximity, dad's best friend, bisexual-awakening romance. Available on AUDIO!

Let Love Win M/M brother's best friend romance. Available on AUDIO!

Buried Secrets Romantic suspense stand-alone title. Available on AUDIO!

Silver in the City (3 books- meet the Silver crew you read about in Forged in the City) Available on AUDIO!

Forged in the City (3 books- a spin-off series from Silver in the City) Available on AUDIO

The BJ Boys Series (3 books, small town, big love) Available on AUDIO

Forever Better Together (friends to lovers) Available on AUDIO!

His Reluctant Cowboy (age gap, opposites attract, cowboy romance) Available on AUDIO!

What Blooms Beneath (LGBT Fantasy romance) Available on AUDIO!

Sawyer

(this was the first M/M I wrote and you may remember Sawyer and Luke being mentioned in <u>Barrett & Ivan</u> as well as in <u>Ryker & Gavin</u>)

❦❦❦

The <u>Something About Him</u> series has been revamped with revised stories, updated blurbs, and spiffy new covers.

The series is available on ALL of your favorite book platforms!

Bryan & Jase

Brody & Nick

Barrett & Ivan

Braeton & Drew

Ryker & Gavin

Kade & Cameron

ABOUT THE AUTHOR

A.D. Ellis is an Indiana girl, born and raised. She spends much of her time in central Indiana as an instructional coach/teacher in the inner city of Indianapolis, being a mom to two amazing teenagers, and wondering how she and her husband of over two decades haven't driven each other insane yet. A lot of her time is also devoted to phone call avoidance and her hatred of cooking.

She loves chocolate, wine, pizza, and naps along with reading and writing romance. These loves don't leave much time for housework, much to the chagrin of her husband. Who would pick cleaning the house over a nap or a good book? She uses any extra time to increase her fluency in sarcasm.

A.D. uses she/they pronouns.

Sign up at http://www.subscribepage.com/ADEllisNewsMMRomance for a FREE books!

Website http://adellisauthor.com/

My direct sale webstore https://payhip.com/ADEllisAuthor

Find me EVERYWHERE at https://www.adellisauthor.com/mylinks/

CONNECT WITH A.D. ELLIS

Follow my website http://www.adellisauthor.com or find me on Facebook

http://www.facebook.com/adellisauthor

If you want to get updates about releases, interviews, sales, giveaways, and more please sign up for my newsletter http://www.subscribepage.com/ADEllisNewsMMRomance

Find me on Spotify if you'd like to listen to the playlist for this book (mainly just the songs I listened to while writing). Just search for A.D. Ellis.

To make it easy, find me EVERYWHERE here- https://www.adellisauthor.com/mylinks/